FUGITIVE LOVE

Belle Bright is on the run. Framed for her husband's murder, she's now being hunted – not only by the police, but also by the real killer. She flees Sydney with her daughters; assuming false identities, they all hide out in a small country town. Belle's new neighbour Sam Taggart becomes her rock, and over time she learns to trust again, even to love. Then her cover is blown, and the murderer arrives in town. Can Belle prove her innocence? And will she survive?

SARAH EVANS

◆

FUGITIVE LOVE

Complete and Unabridged

LINFORD
Leicester

First published in Great Britain in 2020

First Linford Edition
published 2022

*A catalogue record for this book is available
from the British Library.*

ISBN 978–1–4448–4832–8

Published by
Ulverscroft Limited
Anstey, Leicestershire

Printed and bound in Great Britain by
TJ Books Ltd., Padstow, Cornwall

This book is printed on acid-free paper

1

Belle strode along the city terrace pavement quivering with outrage. A hot wind lifted her lemon cotton skirt and whip-cracked her nut-brown hair. She slapped down the skirt and irritably looped the flapping hair behind her ears. She increased her pace, determined to confront her husband before her courage failed.

She should never have come to Australia in the first place. She should have known this so-called adventure wouldn't work. So much for a new beginning in a new country. It was a nightmare and it was time to say goodbye and good riddance. She had the divorce papers in her bag and this time she wouldn't be sweet-talked into staying. She wouldn't be emotionally blackmailed to continue for the children's sake. Oh no, she would march into that damn office and get him to sign those documents with zero negotiation.

Xander had blown his chances once and for all. He'd cheated one too many times, done one too many shonky deals, and Belle was sick to the back teeth of being thrust into constant damage control. She was out of here. Their marriage was finished. She'd pack up their belongings and take the girls back to the UK.

Her husband's office was in a slick glass and steel block that overlooked the Sydney Harbour. She took the elevator to the fifth floor, sharing the lift with a couple of businessmen and a woman in a sharp navy power-suit who oozed capability. Belle wished she could absorb some of the woman's strong confidence. Even a gram of it would have doubled her meagre store. Perhaps she should have worn something more corporate rather than her cool cotton? Well, it was done now.

When the doors swished open, Belle took a deep breath and exited the elevator car. She marched towards Xander's office suite along the empty corridor, her low sandal heels click-clacking loudly, disturbing the muted silence.

At Bright Financial Services, Belle pushed open the heavy door and entered the black and white foyer. Lush pot plants were tastefully placed. There was a wide jarrah desk with a leather lounge off to one side with a coffee table littered with thick glossy magazines to entertain waiting clients. It reeked of sophistication. Yes, thought Belle, Xander was so good at appearances. Shame he couldn't back it up with integrity.

The secretary was absent from her station. Belle wasn't surprised. She was probably out the back, snogging with Xander. That would be about right. Belle bit back a snarl of contempt. It wouldn't be the first time, or the last, and that knowledge fuelled her anger. They were long overdue for this divorce.

While she was getting Xander to sign on the dotted line, Belle would also get him to explain the large amount of money she'd found hidden under the mattress on his side of the bed. For goodness sake, how cliché was that? As if she wouldn't find it!

The A3 orange manilla envelope had been stuffed full of $100 and $50 notes. She hadn't counted them but reckoned on several thousand. She guessed it was dirty money and she was furious with Xander. He'd promised her there would be no more illegal activity. No more cheating. Hah, and she'd believed him. How stupid was that?

Belle didn't bother to knock but cannoned through into Xander's inner sanctum and skidded to a halt. There was a split second as she grappled to comprehend the stark scene before her, and then she screamed.

Xander was lying on the floor in a pool of blood.

Her anger vaporised. She fell to her knees, throwing her tote bag off to one side, and tried to stem the flow. There was so much blood! It gurgled in his throat, soaked his shirt — the same shirt she had ironed only this morning. What a crazy thing to think of now. But it was better than focusing on the blood.

Belle yelled over her shoulder for help. She appealed to Xander to stay with her, to keep conscious. She sobbed as she tugged at his tie and tried to free his airways from the frothing redness filling his mouth and nose, but she couldn't. His head slumped backwards, lifeless. She stared in disbelief at his face, then at her trembling hands; they were covered in his blood.

She lunged for the phone to ring for an ambulance, wasting precious seconds punching in the wrong number with blood-wet fingers; she was in Australia now, not the UK. Get a grip, Belle.

From somewhere behind her she heard a sound. She dropped the phone.

Help? Thank goodness. She swung her head towards the noise. Xander's new business partner Camelo Milo stepped out of the shadows of the neighbouring office.

Their eyes locked. Belle swallowed hard. She didn't think he was there to help her.

The usually sharply dressed man was dishevelled with his tailored black suit jacket hanging open and his pink tie skewed to the left. His face was pale with a sheen of sweat. His dark coiffed hair was mussed. He gave the distinct impression he'd been in a fight.

And then she saw the gun. He was holding it loosely down by his side.

'Camelo?'

'What are you doing here?' There was a distinct edge to his question.

'What happened? Xander's dead!'

He ignored her question as she had ignored his. 'You shouldn't be here.'

'I wanted to see Xander.'

'What a good wife. Xander was a lucky man.'

Hah, thought Belle, he wouldn't have said that if he'd known about the divorce papers in her shoulder bag.

'And you'll make the perfect widow — unless you've just called the cops, because then you'll make the perfect corpse.'

Belle's heart convulsed. This couldn't

be happening! Guns and murder didn't happen to ordinary people like her.

'Did you call the cops, Belle?' He looked at the blood smeared phone.

'No. I tried to call for an ambulance but I couldn't get through.'

'It's too late for an ambulance, darling.' And he laughed. Milo flicked the gun upwards and pointed directly at her. This was unbelievable. How could this be happening? 'Where's my money, Belle?'

She glanced down at her husband's still, bloodied face. So that money burning a hole in her shoulder bag was Milo's? Even in death Xander caused her grief. No surprises there. Her twelve years with him had been a roller coaster ride, with most of that ride heading downhill at breakneck speed. It hadn't been a thrilling ride.

'My money has gone AWOL. It was for a business drop that failed to happen last night. Bright was the last one to have it. The other party is understandably annoyed. I need it today.'

'A drop?'

'Don't play the innocent with me, Belle. I know you're up to the mark with Bright's business dealings. It was cash in exchange for certain . . . recreational goods.' Milo gave a knowing smile and Belle stared back at him.

'I have nothing to do with Xander's work apart from cleaning his office.'

Feeling at a disadvantage on the floor, Belle struggled to her feet. She could feel Xander's blood drying, tightening on her skin. She wanted to wash it off. Instead she rubbed her hands down her skirt.

'You expect me to believe that?' said Milo.

'Why would I lie?' She wrapped her arms around her body, trying to stop herself from shaking. She needed to keep a clear head.

'Bright stole half a million dollars from me and I want it back.' His eyes narrowed and he focussed intently on her. His voice became more demanding. 'I'm not afraid to use this to get it,' and he waved the gun menacingly. 'So give it to me or you and the kids will die. Do you understand?'

'But I don't have it!' Because no way $500,000 was in that envelope. Milo must be alluding to another cache of money, one that she knew nothing about.

'I don't believe you. If you want, we can do this nice and slow. I enjoy a little persuasion.' He gave a harsh laugh. 'I could start with the kids. You can watch. That will be fun, won't it?'

'You're sick,' spat Belle.

'Practical. I want that money and I'll get it, whatever it takes.'

Fear clutched at Belle, but she fought the hysteria. She rapidly scanned the desk to see if there was anything she could use to defend herself. Apart from a cold cup of coffee and a large pebble from Brighton Beach that her eldest daughter had painted as a paperweight for Father's Day, that was it. Xander had always favoured a minimalist office.

'So cough up, darling Belle, and tell me where it is. I know you have it. Your lovely amber eyes betray you.' And he lifted the gun higher. 'Come on, I'm running out of patience.'

'You want it? Well here it is,' Belle leaned across the desk and, grasping the mug, she threw the contents at Milo's face. With her other hand, she lifted the paperweight and swung it up with a swift uppercut that struck Milo hard on the chin as he reared back from the coffee. He crumpled to the floor without a sound.

Belle stared. Heck, she hadn't expected him to fall. She'd thought she'd just glance him, but instead, Milo lay there stunned, blinking, and dripping in coffee. Belle wasn't game to hit him again. Hands shaking, she dropped the rock, scooped up her bag and ran.

The corridor was still empty. She clattered along it and half fell into the elevator. On the ground floor she headed to the nearest restroom. The woman who'd been in the elevator earlier was there touching up her scarlet lipstick. She glanced at Belle's wild-eyed pale face and then at her blood covered clothes and hands.

'Oh my goodness!'

'There's been an accident.' Belle lunged for the sink and ran the tap, frantically washing her hands. Blood mixed with the water and swirled around the basin, turning it pink. She washed her hands again, just to make sure, and tried not to gag as she thought of all that blood and Xander struggling to breathe his last. Or of Milo, lying concussed on the floor.

'I'll call emergency services,' said the woman.

'Please.'

'You OK?'

'No.' And she leaned forward and wretched into the sink, the acid stinging her throat.

The woman put a hand on her shoulder. 'Is there anything I can do to help?'

'Wait for the police and ambulance. Show them where to go — the Bright Financial Services' office on the fifth floor,' Belle said holding hard on the

11

basin to stop herself falling over, wiping her mouth with shaking fingers. 'But don't you go in there. There was a man in there with a gun. He may still be there.'

'What about you? Are you alright to be alone?'

'I'll be OK in a minute. Once the shock has worn off.' Belle convulsively gagged again and the woman took a step backwards.

'If you say so,' she said and awkwardly patted her shoulder again before leaving at a rapid trot.

Once the vomiting stopped, Belle sluiced cold water over her face and dabbed it dry with a paper towel. She hesitated a moment. Should she stay for the police? But then she thought of Milo, of his gun and his threat to hurt the girls. She should have hit him harder. What if he was hunting for her now, this minute?

No. She was out of here.

She headed to their home on a quiet suburban estate. She rapidly packed a few clothes into a single suitcase, collected up their passports and drove to the school. She'd collect the kids and then head to the airport. They'd be home tomorrow. That sounded so good.

Belle parked in a shaded spot and waited impatiently for the school bell. She drummed her fingers on the steering wheel. She took a deep breath and exhaled slowly. There was nothing to be gained by being impatient. Instead of thumping the wheel, she may as well book their flights. She grabbed her phone and spent some time researching flights. Dammit, there weren't any seats until the next evening! What were the odds? They would have to lay low until then and simply pray hard that Milo wouldn't find them.

As the pupils began spilling out of the school gates, Belle slipped out of her car, resting her hip against the wing, and scanned the faces. She waved when she saw her oldest daughter, Hannah, and swiftly went towards her. She hugged her fast before releasing her and saying, 'Go find you sister. We're in a hurry.'

Her tension mounted as she waited

for the girls to appear and then there was Hannah, tugging along a reluctant Elspeth.

'Hannah's being a big bully,' winged Elspeth. 'I was talking to my friend.'

'She was just doing as she was told,' said Belle. She gave Hannah a swift smile and got an eye-roll in reply. 'Come on,' said Belle. 'There's no time to waste.' She piled the girls into the car, ignoring her youngest child's grumbles.

They eased into the stream of cars with Belle mentally cursing the rush hour traffic. With hands clenched on the wheel, she joined the flow of vehicles onto the road that would take them out of the city and off into the wide open country where she reckoned she'd feel safer, where she could breathe and process the horror of the afternoon, and try to work out what to do, how to outwit Milo.

'Where are we going, Mummy?' asked Hannah.

'It's a surprise.' Because Belle didn't have a clue. This was all new to her.

14

She didn't know the roads, the suburbs, the towns. She didn't even know if she was heading north or south. She could barely think. But she had to, for all their sakes. Oh goodness, Xander was dead! It seemed horrifically surreal. Maybe she'd wake up and realise it was just a horrid dream.

'I'm hungry,' said Hannah.

'Did you finish your packed lunch?'

'No.'

'So eat that.'

'But Mum! The cheese is warm and rubbery.'

'Don't argue with me, Hannah. I've got to concentrate on the road. I'll get you something else once we're clear of this awful traffic.'

Her head pounded. All she could think of was her husband lying dead on the floor. Of all that blood. Of Milo with the gun.

'Can I go to Jazzy's house tonight?' asked Elspeth. 'They're having pizza.'

'No. We won't be back in time.' Like ever. Because Xander was dead! What a nightmare.

'But, Mum, she's my new friend,' Elspeth whined. 'I want to go. It'll be fun.'

'No. I'm sorry. I'll explain later. Now hush, I need to concentrate.'

Elspeth didn't and loudly bawled her anger. Hannah shouted at her sister and Belle yelled at both of them with such a ferocious bellow the girls fell silent, awed and a little afraid by their mother's uncharacteristic outburst.

'Good. That's better,' said Belle, reining in her fury. 'Keep it like that.'

She returned her attention to the traffic while a small voice in her head admonished that she shouldn't have run. She should have waited for the police. She should have stayed, found somewhere safe until the police had arrived rather than going off half-cocked. But then there was Milo. Xander had mentioned several times how dangerous he was. She hadn't wanted to take the risk. Belle kept on driving while the girls sat in the back, hunched and miserable.

Much later they pulled into a motel

on the outskirts of the city and booked a room.

'Why are we here?' said Elspeth in a small, fed up voice.

'We're going home,' said Belle.

'To England?' Belle nodded. 'I don't want to.'

'We have to.'

'Has Daddy lost his job again?'

'Something like that.'

'Where is he?'

'He's staying here.' Belle's voice snatched and she turned her back on the girls so they wouldn't see the pain on her face.

'Can't I stay with him?'

'No.'

'Can I watch telly?' asked Hannah.

'Yes.' Belle slumped on the bed, curling into a foetal ball, and and buried her face in her hands, trying to block out the harsh reality engulfing her like a toxic cloud. She could hear Elspeth moaning until she gave up and watched a cartoon with her sister. The programme finished and was followed by the evening news.

'Why are we on TV?' said Elspeth.

Hannah jumped up and down excitedly. 'Gosh, we're famous!' she said clapping her hands.

Belle raised her head from the pillow. A chill went through her. Her own face flashed on the screen. The public were being asked to look out for her as she was wanted for questioning. She was a person of interest in a fatality in the Sydney CBD. Was she wanted for murder? Why hadn't Belle seen that one coming? Because murder and guns didn't involve people like her!

She switched off the television. 'We have to out of here,' she said with stark bluntness.

'Why?' said Elspeth. 'What's a fatality?'

'It means someone's dead,' said Hannah.

'Who?' Elspeth asked.

Belle hesitated and then said, 'There was an accident. Let's go. And be very, very quiet. No one must see us. Do you understand?' Elspeth nodded. Hannah looked doubtful and looked as though she was going to argue. 'Han, don't start, there's a good girl.'

Belle abandoned hopes of flying home. The airport would be watched by police. Instead she drove steadily through the night and in the early hours pulled over into a lay-by. She leaned heavily against the steering wheel and wept in despair, muffling her sobs with her forearm, while her daughters slept on the back seat.

★ ★ ★

A few days later and Belle was seriously questioning her skewed logic. She'd thought that fleeing from the scene, ditching the family car, changing their names, buying cheap wigs to disguise themselves and hiding from Milo and the police had been the only logical thing to do.

What had she been thinking? Had she lost her grip on reality? She'd acted like a madwoman! But it was too late to go back now. The police would think her absence equalled guilt.

After driving across the Nullarbor to reach Western Australia, the adrenaline-fuelled need to keep running petered out. The three of them were exhausted and disorientated. Belle was tired of being upbeat for the girls' sakes, tired of living out of their one suitcase. They needed to find a bolt hole to recuperate and take stock.

In Esperance, she bought some scissors and hair dye and turned them all into shag-cut blondies. They raided the op-shops and kitted themselves out with clothes that were completely different to the ones they usually wore and then they hit the road again.

As they drove through Mooralup in the state's south-west, Belle decided it was as good a place as any to stop. It was a small, pretty town with a wide river, big trees and rolling hills. It seemed so serene and clean after endless dusty roads and desert scrub. And hopefully it would be safe.

'What do you reckon, girls?' said Belle,

trying to be enthusiastic. 'Shall we stay here a while?'

Hannah shrugged. 'I suppose.'

Elspeth peered out of the window. 'It looks lonely,' she said and Belle wondered if she was projecting her own feeling of isolation.

'I think it will do. At least for the time being.'

Belle cruised the main street and parked outside the small real estate agents. She left the girls in the car while she enquired if there were any cheap rentals. As luck would have it, there was a shearers' cottage several kilometres out of town that was in her price range. She took it, sight unseen, and paid cash for the bond from Xander's envelope. The agent gave her a scrap of paper with the directions for the property scrawled on it and a large iron key. Belle collected some groceries before following the basic directions to the house.

The cottage was a tired weatherboard house with peeling white paint. The roof was rusty corrugated tin that dipped ominously in places. The verandah was low slung with drooping floorboards that had suffered from too many wet winters and blistering hot summers. The harsh, dry garden with straggling roses and scorched wild rye grass did nothing to help the oppressive air of sad neglect.

There were a few saving graces — a massive plumbago bush, dusted with delicate pale blue flowers, monopolised one side of the garden, and a bold morning glory vine bear-hugged the toilet and laundry outhouse's wooden walls with its lush royal blue blooms.

Then there was the massive oak tree. It cast a wide welcome shade over the house during the hot, still afternoon, drowning it in dappled gold and green coolness. It was a poignant reminder of Belle's home. Home that was twelve thousand miles away. Home that she hadn't wanted to leave but had done so to salvage her floundering marriage. So much for her sacrifice.

Inside, the cottage was surprisingly clean with basic furniture and kitchen utensils, though there was no linen to speak of, just a ratty hand towel by the kitchen sink. They ate a picnic tea, which once upon a time would have been a novelty but was now commonplace, and then they rolled out their sleeping bags and cuddled together in the one old double bed that smelled of stale dust and fresh rodent.

Tomorrow they would start piecing together their new life — airing the mattress would be the number one priority.

2

A stray hand plucked at Belle's sleeve. She flinched as hot panic seared through her. Her instant response was to hit out and run!

Instead, against her fight or flight instincts, she held her ground. She was through with running. No one could find them here. At least that was the sincere hope.

'Hello, dear,' said the woman who had accosted her. 'You're new to town, aren't you?'

Belle clamped down on her clattering heart. She stretched her lips into a semblance of a smile, attempting to hide the residue of fear pounding through her nervous system from the woman's unexpected touch.

'Yes.' She didn't offer further information and would have moved away if it hadn't been for the hand resting on her arm. The woman, with iron-grey hair and a blue floral dress reminiscent of the fifties, smiled with a welcoming but definitely questioning air. Belle didn't want this nosy-parker pumping her for information.

'Ah, I thought so. A tourist wouldn't be buying up big on toilet rolls,' the woman laughed.

Not for the first time, Belle questioned her own sanity. Why had she chosen to hide in this small country town? How could she have thought that her little family would be invisible here? A city would have given them anonymity. No one would have cared who they were, what they were doing or why they were doing it. In this tight-knit community of Mooralup all that, and so much more, was of prime concern to the inhabitants.

Belle could almost hear the native drums cranking up, but apart from rudely galloping off into the fresh produce aisle, Belle was stuck with her smiling inquisitor. 'We arrived last week,' she said and made to walk on, except the woman tugged at her sleeve.

'You'll find us friendly mob,' she said. 'And there's so much to do here. You'll be part of the community in no time.'

Over my dead body! And Belle would be dead too, if she raised her head too high.

'I think we'll take it quietly to begin with, just until we find our feet,' Belle said politely.

'Very sensible. Get a feel of the place. You have children?'

'Yes.'

'Lovely. How old are they?'

'Primary school age,' Belle said, purposefully vague. She wasn't going to be handing out details. The less known about them the better.

'This is a good place to raise a family.'

'I'm sure.' But she wouldn't be here for long. Just enough time to get themselves organised.

'Which school will they be going to? My daughter works at the state primary. That's a nice little school. Friendly.'

'I haven't got around to enrolling them yet.'

'Best get on to it, before the Easter holidays.'

'Yes. I will. Soon.'

Belle hoped the town's interest in them would die down, and then they could begin to claw back their lives, perhaps regain some normality — if only she could remember what normal was. Since Xander's death she'd been in free fall. But if the likes of this woman persisted with her endless probing questions, Belle would be forced to hit the road again. She simply couldn't risk blowing their cover. She had to protect her girls from Camelo Milo, in case he made good his threat to hurt and maybe kill them.

The woman kept on, her gimlet eye focussed on Belle. Belle fielded the questions as best she could before her nerve finally failed her and she escaped through the check-out with only half the things she'd intended to buy.

Belle haphazardly slung her shopping into the boot of her dusty brown station-wagon. The old car had served them well. She'd had her doubts when she'd bought it in Esperance, but it had kept rumbling along, cruising over the dirt roads like an old couch on well-oiled coasters.

Belle swiped at the perspiration beading her forehead. Sweat trickled between her breasts. She couldn't get used to the relentless heat. The flies, the glare, the wide open space. It was taking time to acclimatise. She yearned to return home to chilly days and grey skies.

'Mrs Carlson!'

Belle froze in the act of throwing a packet of toilet rolls into the car. She twisted around, clutching the rolls to her chest as the familiar panic roared through her. A tall, raw-boned man in a slouch hat was regarding her steadily.

Get a grip! she admonished herself. Because this was no assassin out to get her. This bloke, in his faded jeans and equally faded checked shirt, looked nothing like a hit man. More home-spun hayseed on the TV show *A Farmer Wants a Wife*. Or a Wild West cowboy throwback.

The man's eyes narrowed at Belle's heightened colour. 'I'm sorry,' he said. 'I didn't mean to scare you. I'm your neighbour. Sam Taggart.'

Belle relaxed her death-grip on the toilet roll and, with her shaking hand, she shook his proffered one — big and hard and rough, a worker's hand.

'You didn't,' she lied and quickly disengaged herself from his warm, firm grip, aware her own hand was disgustingly sweaty.

He quirked an eyebrow, as though he'd caught on she'd lied.

'How did you know my name?' she asked.

'Patty Clarke told me. She said you'd taken over the Swifts' old shearers cottage.'

'Patty Clarke?'

He indicated the supermarket. 'You were talking to her a moment ago.'

'Oh. I didn't catch her name.'

'That's not like Patty. She's usually quick to introduce herself.' He gave the impression he was trying not to smile.

'Perhaps she did and I wasn't paying attention.'

'Ah.' His eyes twinkled. 'That would be it.'

Belle resumed her cack-handed stowing away of her purchases, hurriedly emptying the shopping trolley, tossing the toilet rolls into the car and then grabbing a weighty plastic bag full of food tins. The bag split and the cans bounced on the bitumen and rolled in all directions.

'Steady,' said the man and he squatted down to retrieve a couple of baked bean cans that had disappeared under the Holden.

Belle scrambled for the other tins in the gutter and chucked them in the back of the car. 'Thank you. But I must be going.'

'You're in a hurry.' It was a flat statement, nothing to get worried about but Belle bridled. What was it to him if she was in a hurry or not?

She squeezed down on her spurt of

anger. It wasn't his fault. He had no idea the pressure she was under. He was being friendly, like that old biddy in the supermarket with her probing questions, and like the other town people who kept trying to chat to her. Keep it cool, she told herself, or you'll lose it big time and then where will you be? In jail, that's where!

She attempted to lighten her tone and, pushing up her fake lens glasses that were slipping down her nose on an oil slick of perspiration, said, 'Yes. There's so much to do. I'm still unpacking.'

Which was another big fat lie. Belle and the kids had only that one suitcase between them. It had taken her just a few minutes to hang and fold the clothes in the cheap, musty wardrobe and drawers of their new home.

'Well, before you go, I'd like to offer my help. That old house you're renting hasn't been lived in for a while. If you need a hand with anything — repairs and the like — just give me a call. I'd be happy to help out.'

'I'll be fine. Thanks.'

'I'm sure you will be, Mrs Carlson,' he said with a touch of irony. 'But the offer still stands.' He regarded her for a long moment and Belle wondered if her abruptness made him suspicious.

Again she tried to modulate her voice. 'I really don't need anything, but thanks anyway, Mr, er . . . '

'Taggart. Sam Taggart.'

'Mr Taggart.'

'I live just over the other side of the paddock from you. If you need me, just holler.'

'You're that close you'd hear?'

'Yep. 'Fraid so. So keep the music down.' His face finally relaxed into a smile.

Belle blinked. The smile didn't just engage his mouth but creased the lines around his eyes and dimpled his cheeks, making him look ten years younger than the forty-plus she'd presumed he was. Any self respecting mature man like that had no business with dimples! They were far too dangerous. But, for heaven's sakes, why was she even noticing? It didn't matter if the man had dimples or not. She had more important things to contend with. Like staying alive, keeping hidden, working out an escape plan.

'Thanks, then. I'll bear that in mind.'

Belle slid into the driver's seat and winced as the sun-hot vinyl burned through her thin pink dress. She was aware of Sam Taggart's scrutiny as she gunned the engine and pulled away up the high street.

OK, so it was nice of the farmer to offer, but she didn't want anything from anybody. All she wanted to do was curl into a tight ball and sleep for eternity. Her exhaustion, fuelled by endless fear, was taking its toll. But of course, she couldn't do that. There were Hannah and Elspeth to consider.

Or Annie and Bess as they were now called. And she was Ria. Ria Carlson. A single mum, and not a widow on the run for murder.

Belle drove in tense concentration along the dirt road to the rental property. She was still getting used to the wide red roads with the ball bearing gravel that caused the Holden to slide dangerously around bends and covered everything with a coat of terracotta dust.

She parked the old car under the oak tree and killed the engine. She took a moment to let the sudden silence ripple around her frayed sanity. She slipped off her plain lens glasses and sagged forward, resting her throbbing head on the steering wheel. She closed her tired eyes. They were scratchy and dry from the sleepless nights, lying in the dark, worrying. She let the peace of the afternoon slowly seep into her bone weary body, so that if felt heavy and slumberous.

How on earth had it come to this? Everything was such a terrible mess! But what else could she have done? *Stayed and faced the police, that's what*, said her inner voice. Well, it was too late for that. She had to make the best of it, for all their sakes. But what was for the best?

★ ★ ★

Sam Taggart whistled through his teeth. That new neighbour of his was one edgy chick. She needed a few corners knocked off of her before she'd fit into their laid-back Mooralup community. If she wanted to fit in, that was, which he very much doubted.

He coughed and waved his hand in front of his face as the ancient Holden took off in a cloud of black smoke. That old bomb was in dire need of a service. But both the woman and the car were none of his business. He wasn't one to go searching out trouble and that Mrs Carlson looked like trouble with a capital T. Sam wasn't after complications. Nope, not him. Not ever.

As he turned to go his saw a couple of stray food cans lying in the Holden's vacated parking space that they had missed. Oh, hell! He scratched the back of his head, dislodging his hat. He readjusted it and bent to collect up the rogue cans. Maybe he'd be seeing his prickly neighbour sooner rather than later. He had hoped it wouldn't be at all.

'Hey, Mum!' Hannah, all long coltish legs in her blue shorts and sleeveless yellow T-shirt, galloped down the steps towards the car. Belle raised her head and stared sleepily. Her momentary peace was over over. 'Thank goodness you're back!'

'What's up, Han?' Belle said as she nudged open the car door and blinked back her tiredness.

'We just found a humongous spider! Come look. It's freaked out Elspeth. She's hiding under the kitchen table like a scaredy-cat!'

Belle went to the boot and hefted it open. She began collecting up the shopping as her daughter bounced up and down and grabbed her arm.

'You've got to catch it and save us!'

'Why me? You could do it. Here, take these bags.' She handed two of the lighter bags to Hannah before slinging one over her own shoulder.

Hannah swung the bags around like a windmill as she talked excitedly. 'It's massive and hairy. A tarantula! I'm not going anywhere near it.'

'So Elspeth's not the only one freaked out, hmm?' Belle laughed and shook her head. 'Let's get this stuff inside before I deal with the beast.'

The spider was a beast too.

The three of them stared at the huge hairy legged creature spanning the bedroom light switch. Elspeth clutched Belle's skirt, Hannah hovered just behind her, ready to run.

Belle had dealt with spiders in the bath back in England, but this was in a class of its own. Was it poisonous? It certainly looked like it, which meant Belle wasn't game to handle it either.

While they contemplated how they were going to relocate the arachnid, they heard a rattle of a vehicle coming into the yard. Belle tensed and moved into the kitchen. She held her finger up to her lips Ssh . . . The girls froze and looked fearfully towards the front door. A car door slammed.

'Mrs Carlson!' There was a bang on

back door. 'Mrs Carlson? Are you there?'

Sam Taggart! Belle slumped in relief. 'Here,' she called, annoyed her voice had an element of neediness.

He was framed in the doorway. 'You look as though you seen a ghost. Is everything OK?'

'No!' said Elspeth, wide-eyed. 'There's a giant tarantula in the bedroom. I'm scared.'

'A tarantula, eh? Do you mean a huntsman?'

'Whatever. It's huge. Take it away,' said Hannah. 'It's horrible!'

'Yes. Take it away,' said Elspeth.

'But don't kill it,' said Belle.

He looked at the three blondies, They were staring at him with large scared eyes and he smiled with amusement at their barrage of orders. 'Any other instructions, ladies?'

'You said you wanted to help. This is your first neighbourly duty,' said Belle with an involuntary smile that disappeared almost immediately. 'I'm embarrassed to say this uninvited visitor is beyond me. Please deal with it.'

'Yes, ma'am.' He quirked a look at Hannah. 'You going to show me where it is, young lady?'

'This way,' said Hannah. 'It's in the bedroom.'

Sam cast a questioning glance at Belle. She shrugged. It wasn't as if there was anything embarrassing to see in there.

He followed Hannah and flicked a glance around the basic room. Three cheap nylon sleeping bags were stretched out on a double bed with a honey-coloured chipped veneer headboard that hailed from the fifties. There was hardly anything else in the room except for a small unpainted chair with a child's shirt draped over it.

'There's the monster.' The girl, who Sam guessed to be about ten or eleven to the other's six or seven, pointed to the spider. It had moved to the ceiling cornice.

'Can you fetch me the broom, kiddo?'

'On it.' Hannah trotted out of the room.

'Why are you here?' Belle asked from behind him. He twisted around to face her, wondering at her abruptness. She was more tense than a coiled spring and her big amber eyes watchful, and she wasn't eye-balling the spider, either. He was the cause of her concern, he realised.

'When you drove away from the supermarket I saw a couple more cans of food in the road. They must have rolled under the car. I thought I'd drop them off on my way home.'

'That's kind of you. Thank you, but you needn't have worried.'

'I wasn't worried.' He glimmered a smile. 'I was happy to oblige.'

Belle wasn't. She felt uncomfortable bringing a stranger into their fugitive world. The less they mixed with people the better.

Hannah marched importantly back into the room with a ratty-headed broom held in her hands like a sword. She presented it to Sam with a small flourish. He took it with a bow. He then gently coaxed the huntsman on to the brush's bristles and carried it outside with little Elspeth squealing from the safety of the verandah.

'All done,' he said, giving Hannah back the broom. 'We should introduce ourselves. I'm Sam Taggart from the next door farm.' He took off his hat, revealing a shock of wild blonde hair, and smiled at the two freckle-faced girls.

Both of them stared back with suddenly stricken, guilty expressions and Belle quickly waded in. 'Annie and Bess,' she said.

And both girls nodded confirmation and smiled in duplicate relief. Belle got the feeling that their response wasn't lost on Sam Taggart.

'Right,' he said, slapping back on his hat. He rifled in his wallet. 'Look, here's my phone number.' He handed Belle a dog-eared business card. 'I'm at your disposal if you get any other unwanted guests, regardless of how many legs they have.'

Belle wondered how he would feel

if she took him at his word and called him out if Camelo Milo turned up. She prayed his offer would never be put to the test. She shivered as if someone had stomped over her grave in size twelve boots.

'Let's hope we don't get any,' she said.

'Well, if you do, I'm here. I'll get those cans from the truck.'

'Stay here girls,' Belle said and followed him.

He handed her the cans of baked beans, sweetcorn and tomatoes. 'If you want fresh tomatoes,' he said, giving the tinned tomatoes a brief shake. 'I have loads growing. Don't stand on ceremony. Just come over and pick them when you want to. I've silver beet and zucchinis too. There's plenty to spare and I'm happy to share.'

'That's kind of you.'

'It's what us neighbours do. I'll be seeing you, Mrs Carlson.' And he waved as he drove off.

* * *

That afternoon Belle and the girls worked on making the cottage more homely. They cleaned the rooms and brought in a bunch of glory vine to put in a jam jar for the the middle of the table. It looked almost cheerful and Belle felt a slight lifting of spirits. Perhaps things were going to be alright after all.

Later, they were having afternoon tea on the verandah when Sam Taggart drove in again.

'Honestly,' she muttered under her breath. 'What does he want now?' And she reluctantly rose to her feet to greet him.

'I'm not staying,' he said, more than aware of the tense vibe of the three females. 'I'm just dropping off some bed linen. I couldn't help but notice you only had sleeping bags. These are surplus to requirements and will be a bit cooler for these warm nights.' He hefted a striped laundry bag full of sheets and dropped it on to the verandah. 'And there are these too.' He passed the girls three pillows. 'And these.' He gave Belle a bag of blankets. 'Which you'll need soon when the nights get chilly, and that won't be far off now that autumn's knocking at summer's door.'

'I don't know what to say,' said Belle, no longer as tense, her voice wobbling. 'Why are you being so kind?' She could feel a shimmer of sudden tears and blinked rapidly. She hadn't expected strangers to be nice to her. She'd felt so alone during these days on the run, but this unlooked for kindness was almost her undoing. She tried desperately to hold on to her brittle composure.

'As I said earlier, we're neighbours, Mrs Carlson, and a little neighbourly kindness never goes amiss.'

'I can't tell you how nice it is.' And she sniffed despite her good intentions to show no emotion.

'No big deal.' His voice was surprisingly gentle.

'Oh but it is,' she said in a rush. 'You have no idea. Thank you. Thank you so much.'

His eyebrows twitched upwards in

response to the throb of emotion in her voice. He tipped his hat. 'I'll be seeing you all.'

'Aren't you going to stay for a cup of tea?' asked Hannah and Belle stiffened.

'We've got chocolate biscuits,' said Elspeth, holding up a plate of half-melting Tim Tams.

'Well, I must say, that would be nice, but only if it's not intruding.'

'Of course not,' said Belle, her body language signalling the complete opposite.

Sam Taggart was no fool. He could read the signs. 'Actually, let's take a rain-check. I have some things that need to get done before dusk. But thanks for the offer,' he said.

Sam wondered why he was bothering to be friendly. He had better things to do with his time than babysit his distrustful neighbours.

3

The heavy stillness of the hot night melted Belle's bones but not her thoughts. She lay flat on her back between her two girls in the creaky double bed. Roll on yet another night of sleeplessness. Though emotionally exhausted, Belle just couldn't relax enough to succumb to oblivion. Her eyes were wide open to the moon, which shone brazenly through the uncurtained windows and cast a silver wash over the bed and chair, gilding all the surfaces and causing deep shadowed pools to fill with blackness. It was an unfamiliar landscape, alien and scary. She missed home. It was hard to think of this barren cottage as their home now.

She thought of home, so far away, and of her family. On cue the familiar panic rose in her gut. Would she ever see them again? What if they were stuck here forever? What if the police found them and she went to jail because she was unable to prove her innocence? What would happen to the girls? And, worse, what if Milo found them?

Would he hurt them? Or even kill them? Belle tried to block her spiralling anxiety by counting her breaths, but the craziness inside her head overrode her sensible side. She couldn't help it, she had the horror of the past few weeks on continuous loop, going round and round her brain.

Her hands curled into fists as she tried to quell the gathering panic. She didn't want to waken the girls by having a meltdown. She gritted her teeth but it didn't stop the tears. They trickled down her face, dampening her hair and pillow. She willed herself to be still, not to give in to this living nightmare.

And then she heard it. A metallic scraping.

Her eyes flew to the window. She'd locked all the doors and windows, despite the stifling heat, as she wasn't brave enough to leave them open.

The scritch-scratching continued.

Someone was trying to break in. Milo? He'd found them?

Fear paralysed her. The noise continued in steady short bursts until she could bear it no longer. She carefully climbed over Elspeth and slipped out of bed. Pulling jeans over her night shirt, she scoped out the front and back of the cottage but couldn't see anything in the moonlight. But she could hear them!

She tip-toed back, collected the Holden keys and then woke the girls, admonishing them to be quiet. She guided the sleepy children out of the house and into the car — then she drove like the clappers!

★　★　★

Headlights flooded his bedroom. Sam woke with a start. What the devil? He heard the clunk of a heavy car door. Then a rapid tattoo on his fly-screened front door. 'Mr Taggart! Mr Taggart!'

He bolted from his bed and wrenched open the door, turning on the verandah

48

light as he did so.

Three pairs of huge, frightened eyes gazed up at him. 'There's someone breaking into our house,' said Belle, her face white and pulled, her voice shaky.

'That's insane.' Serious crime didn't happen in Mooralup. And if there was an intruder, which he sincerely doubted, why would they target that ramshackle cottage? It didn't make sense. Which then begged the question, was Ria Carlson actually expecting someone to break in? Hah, that was his guess. She was too secretive by half.

'But true all the same,' said Belle. 'Can we stay here? Please? I know it's a big ask but I'm frightened.' Her voice had an edge of hysteria.

'Of course.' He took in the dazed, sleepiness of the little girls. 'Come on in.' He ushered them into the cool house.

'Lock the door . . . please.' Belle said fearfully.

'OK' Before he did, he looked around the yard. Everything was dead quiet, except for the tick-tick of the Holden engine and the singing of the frogs. He slammed the door and shot the bolts to keep her happy.

'All secure. Come into the kitchen.' He snapped on the light and then realised his state of undress. He grabbed a tea towel and wrapped it around his boxers, holding it firmly in one hand. He picked up his phone with the other. 'I'll call the police.'

'No!' Shrieked Belle. 'No police!'

He gave her a puzzled look. 'But if there's an intruder they need to know so they can investigate and catch the bugger.'

'No. Please. I don't want the police involved.'

Her eyes were huge tawny pools of fear and desperation.

'OK then.' But he didn't sound convinced. He put the phone down. 'So how about I make up my bed for you all to sleep in?'

'We can sleep on the lounge floor.'

'That's not going to happen, Mrs Carlson. It's my bed or nothing.'

50

'We couldn't oust you from your bed.'

'The girls are dead on their feet and you'll be more comfortable all together. It's what you're used to . . . Think of the girls.'

Belle pursed her lips. 'If you're sure?' She held the girls tight within the circle of her arms. The three of them looked shell-shocked. What had they endured to make them this terrified? Sam couldn't even begin to hazard.

'I'm positive. It's no sweat.' He did a quick bed strip but not before he pulled on his jeans and a work shirt. He came out of the bedroom and dumped the soiled sheets in the laundry and collected clean ones. The Carlsons followed him back to the master bedroom. They hovered in the doorway. When he shook out the clean sheets, Belle stepped forward and caught the other side and helped him make up the bed.

He couldn't help but notice how thin she was as she tugged at the fitted sheet. Her jeans bagged around her hips and her breasts were just about non-existent under her T-shirt — not that he was particularly looking.

'I'm sorry about all this,' said Belle. 'But I was scared. I didn't know what to do. And you did say . . . ' Her voice cracked.

'It's no trouble, Mrs Carlson. And to put your mind at rest, I'll lock the rest of the doors and windows and I'll keep a watch out till morning.'

'I'm so very, very grateful.' There was a shimmer in her eyes, but she blinked back the tears. 'Thank you.'

Later, when they were all settled and Sam could hear their measured slow breathing of deep sleep, he stood silently in the open doorway of his bedroom. He gazed down at the tousled blondes, especially the mother. Good grief, how had it come to this? He never had women in his house, had never encouraged it, and now this fragile, prickly woman was not only in his house but in his bed!

It didn't sit well with him, but what else could he have done? The farm was his refuge. Seems it was now Ria Carlson's and her girls' refuge too.

The woman must have been damned afraid to come running to him. He hadn't seen her for weeks. So what was Ria Carlson's secret? Why was she running scared? And did he really even want to know?

He decided not to answer his own question.

★ ★ ★

Belle hugged the sleeping girls close to her. She kissed them both on their heads. Inexplicably, she felt safe for the first time since Xander's murder. As she lay there on the crisp, sweet-smelling cotton, her tightly coiled body began to unfurl and relax. She could feel the warmth permeating through from the mattress where Sam had lain minutes before. That was curiously comforting. She nestled down in the darkness. The tension in her neck and shoulder muscles slowly released. Her stomach stopped cramping. Her eyelids fluttered shut. Moments later she fell into a deep and dreamless sleep.

The Carlsons slept in late. Sam, though tired from his disturbed night, was up and about at dawn. He left them a note telling them to help themselves to breakfast. When he returned there was still no sign of them. He made himself a coffee and sat down at the kitchen table and got on with farm paperwork while he waited for them to emerge.

A while later a sleepy Belle stumbled into the room. Her bleached hair spiked untidily, her eyes were blurry and vacant. She looked soft and vulnerable and as sweet as melted marsh-mellow. There wasn't a sharp edge or prickle in sight.

She gave him a tentative smile. 'Morning.'

He responded with his own smile of welcome. 'Sleep well?'

'Best sleep I've had in ages.' Her voice was slumber-husky and relaxed.

Sam opened his mouth to ask why, only to clamp it shut again. *Remember, you fool, you don't need to know, you don't want to know.* The Carlsons were none of his business.

'Would you like breakfast or go straight into lunch?' he said to change to the subject.

'Is it that late?'

'It sure is, lady.'

'I suppose we should go back to the cottage.' But she didn't sound at all keen.

'I went over this morning.'

'You did?' Her eyes widened in trepidation.

'I had Derek with me — the dog. And everything was fine. Nothing had been disturbed, except for the kitchen.'

Her eyes widened further.

'What did they do?' And her hands clenched at her side, as if to stop them shaking.

'They had a party. There was a bit of a mess, but I evicted your intruder without much trouble.'

'You did? Golly, that was brave of you!'

'Not really. He was as dozy as hell. Or I should say she.' And he grinned at her puzzled expression. 'You had a possum down the chimney, Mrs Carlson. She was looking for a comfortable place to hunker down with her baby.'

'A possum?' She didn't sound convinced. 'But I heard someone trying to break in!'

'It was most probably the possum testing the roof iron, seeing if she could weasel her way into the attic. Instead she chose the easier option of the chimney. There was soot, ash and droppings all over your floor but I cleaned it up. You home is relatively liveable once more.'

'A possum.' Her shoulders sagged. 'I didn't even think of that. I just shot straight into panic mode. What an idiot! I'm so sorry. I can't begin to thank you enough, Mr Taggart.'

'No worries. So . . . ' He smiled broadly, 'breakfast or lunch?'

'Tea and toast would be nice, thank you.'

While Sam fixed it, he was aware of her eyes roving around the barrack-style kitchen, analysing his surroundings, taking an inventory. Ria Carlson didn't look comfortable in his bachelor pad, but then she seldom appeared relaxed, period, and he felt awkward too. This woman was unsettling with her air of fragility and sweetness overlaid with her throbbing vibe of tension and fear.

'It's very . . . ' began Belle.

'Utilitarian?' Sam swept his kitchen a look. It was sparsely furnished with no extra trimmings. There was an unlit slow combustion stove with a well-used armchair next to it with bald arm rests, a long farmhouse-style table with six mismatched wooden chairs, a kitchenette, a couple of sideboards and a Welsh dresser that displayed four mugs and a blue china setting for one.

'Yes. No nonsense.'

'It's how I like it. It's easy to keep clean.'

'True. My kitchen's the same.'

'But not through choice, I guess.' Now why did he say that? He didn't want to know. Didn't want to get involved.

'No.' She didn't elaborate, which didn't surprise him. She would share in her own sweet time, if ever. 'So you live alone, Mr Taggart?'

'What does it look like?' He'd been on his own for a few years. His choice. There was always company if he wanted it, but not at the farm. This was his sanctuary.

She shrugged. 'Don't you get lonely out here on your own?'

He placed the tea and toast on the table. 'Nope. It suits me just fine, lady.' He added butter and honey. 'I can do what I want, when I want, and not answer to anyone.'

'Sounds perfect.'

'It is. I'll be out in the barn if you want me.'

Once in the barn, Sam picked up the spanner and stared at the tractor engine, replaying the conversation. It was true, he liked being alone. He didn't get lonely, at least not often. But now he felt unsettled. Which he hadn't felt in a long time. Hmm. The sooner the Carlson family left, the better for his peace of mind.

4

A week or so later, at breakfast, Belle took the kettle to the sink. She turned on the cold tap. Only a dribble of water came out. She tried the hot and it ran for a little while before stopping too. What was going on?

'Mummy, the toilet won't flush,' said Hannah.

'Ew gross,' said Elspeth. 'But I need to go.'

'There's no water in the taps either,' said Belle, frowning.

'Why not?'

'I have no idea, Han.' And she didn't. In her old life you just turned on a tap and, hey presto, water spurted out.

Belle hadn't given the cottage's water supply much thought. She knew the pressure was lousy, regardless if the tap was turned on full or not, but she hadn't thought any further than that. Perhaps it had something to do with the rusty tank that sat on top of a man-made mound a hundred metres or so from the house?

'I'll go and investigate,' she said without conviction, not sure what she was actually investigating, but feeling she had to do something.

She climbed up the red clay hillock. The morning sun had a bite already, burning her arms and beating down on her bare head. There was no way she could see inside the tank and so she tapped the galvanised corrugated iron. The tank sounded hollow. Oh dear. She didn't think that was a good sign.

OK, so now what? She didn't have a clue. She sighed. She would have to ask the cowboy from next door for help. Again.

She trudged over the straw-coloured mown paddock, weaving between the large rolls of baled hay, to look for Sam Taggart.

Sam was working on an engine in his barn with the double doors wide open. His old Kelpie raised his head and barked. Sam cast a look over his shoulder and saw the slight form of his edgy young neighbour crossing his yard, looking wide-eyed and a little apprehensive. She was in her ill-fitting jeans and a pink T-shirt. She didn't look much older than her kids.

And she wasn't wearing her glasses. Yet again.

He wandered to the barn entrance, wiping his black oily hands on a rag that wasn't much cleaner than his hands. 'Mrs Carlson. What can I do for you today?'

She jumped and regrouped. 'Mr Taggart.' She wrapped her arms around herself in a defensive gesture. 'I'm sorry to bother you so early but I have a problem.'

Of course she did. Her whole life was a problem and it seemed to keep involving him, which meant she was his problem. Well, it was his fault. He'd initially offered his help and now he was duty-bound to deliver.

'What sort of problem?'

'There's no water.'

'Have you tried turning on the pump?'

'Pump?'

'You do know you have to pump the water from the bore into the tank to feed into the house?'

'Bore?'

He regarded her for a long moment and tried not to sigh in exasperation. 'OK, I'll come and take a look.'

'Thank you. I'd appreciate that.' She turned to walk back the way she'd come.

'Wait there, Mrs Carlson. We'll take the ute.'

'We will?'

'I'll need my tools in case the pump is broken. We'll take some water too, just in case. I expect the girls are thirsty.'

She followed him to the cool farm-house. In the laundry, he gave his hands a thorough soapy wash and then from a cupboard he unearthed a small foam covered drinks esky that had seen a lot of use, judging by the battered dirty blue polystyrene. Sam rinsed it out and shoved it under the tap.

He glanced at Belle while he waited for it to fill. 'No more intruders?' he said.

'No. Look, I'm sorry I over reacted the

other night. I'm not usually that flaky. It's been a bad time for me.'

'You don't have to explain a thing.' He turned off the tap and screwed the esky lid in place. 'Come on. Let's get back to your girls.'

Back at the cottage, Belle gave the girls a drink from the esky and then filled the kettle to make tea for Sam Taggart and herself. It gave her something to do while he loomed large in her kitchen, filling it with his coiled, earthy energy.

'So the agent didn't inform you how the pump and tanks operated when you hired the place?' He looked at the brew as she set it down on the old scratched green Formica-topped table. He was a coffee man, but he let it slide.

'No. And I didn't ask. I just presumed we were on mains water. Naive of me, I realise now. But I had no idea.'

'I'll have a word with them. They should have explained to you what to do. That manager's a real slack buggar.'

'Please don't say anything. I really don't want to make a fuss.' Or draw attention. The less she had to do with the town's people the better.

He shrugged. 'Your call.'

He drank the tea under sufferance and then spent the morning fixing the pump. Once it was working, he turned it on to refill the tank from the bore. It was a learning curve for both Belle and the girls.

'We drink water from the ground?' Hannah wrinkled her nose. 'How gross.'

'Be grateful you have water,' he said.

'So can I flush the toilet now?' said Elspeth.

'You may, little one.'

'Would you like to have lunch with us, Mr Taggart?' Belle asked. 'I was going to make some bacon butties.'

He gave her a quizzical look.

'I was unforgivably rude the other day. I should have insisted you stayed for a cuppa,' she said with a rush. 'I'm more mentally prepared today.'

'Really?'

'No.' And she offered him a nervous half smile. 'But the offer of lunch still

64

stands.'

He had things to do but he didn't want to knock back her tentative olive branch. If they were going to be neighbours, it was better they got on. Or at least that was his logic. The fact he was prepared to hang out with the Carlsons at all was beside the point, but he didn't want to go there.

'Well, bacon butties sound delicious,' he said.

He washed his hands and sat down at the green Formica-topped table and cast around for something to say that wouldn't send her into a tailspin. 'No more spiders?'

'Not big ones.'

'The small ones can be poisonous.'

'I don't think I'll be calling you out for every spider we see, Mr Taggart,' she retorted.

The irony wasn't lost on him that he felt that was a shame. It would have been an excuse to come around. It had been a while since he'd sat at a table and let a woman who was easy on the eye fix him lunch. *Don't go there!*

'Well, you girls watch out for redbacks and whitetails. They're nasty critters.'

'Did you hear that, girls?'

They both nodded, looking like fat-cheeked hamsters as they munched their sandwiches.

'I expect you'll be enrolling them in school?'

'Soon.' She didn't elaborate and he felt he'd overstepped the mark. Jeez, it was hard passing the time of day with this woman!

Lunch was a quiet affair. The girls were big-eyed and mute, concentrating on their food while watching his every move. It wasn't restful and didn't offer much in the way of conversation. He ate his butty as fast as politeness dictated, declined another cup of tea and left.

★ ★ ★

Belle watched him hustle out the door. Well, that had gone well, she didn't think!

But did it matter? No, Farmer

66

Taggart could keep to his side of the fence, unless there was an emergency. And then she twisted her lips in a self deprecating smile. She hated to admit it, but she did like knowing he was close by. She just didn't want to feed him too often.

Belle cleared up the lunch debris and washed the dishes. She stared out the window, thinking.

It had been six weeks now since Xander's death. Six weeks since she'd had contact with her family. Should she call them? Would they have left any messages? Belle had sent her mum a text message when they had fled Sydney, telling her they would be away for a spell and that she'd ring once they got back home. She hadn't touched the phone since then, just in case the police could track her. But surely it would be safe to check the messages?

Girding her courage, Belle switched on the phone and clicked on messages . . .

Where's my money, tramp?

Belle dropped the phone and stared in

disbelief. Camelo Milo had her number? How?

She held her hand against her chest and sucked in deep breaths. She stared at the phone as though it was radioactive. After a moment, she tentatively picked it up and began to scroll down the messages . . .

Where are you, tramp?
I will find you.
You're dead!

Belle shut down the phone.

She felt sick to the pit of her stomach and instinctively turned her gaze towards Sam Taggart's farm. She could confide in him, tell him how scared she was. But who was she kidding? How stupid. As if he could help. She couldn't share this with him, or anyone else for that matter. She was on her own.

5

Sam Taggart spotted the two Carlson girls in the farm lane and stopped his ute. He passed them most mornings as they walked to the highway, with their bulky backpacks slung over their shoulders, to catch the orange school bus. They'd been attending school for a couple of weeks now.

'How's it going girls?' he asked.

'Fine, thanks, Mr Taggart,' said Hannah with wary politeness. She was like any other schoolgirl, except she didn't smile very often. And neither did the little one. It wasn't right. He knew first-hand that childhood could be grim, but he wished he could discover the reason for their sad reserve. It wasn't as if he could ask their mum. Ria Carlson didn't invite confidences and he actually hadn't seen her much since that awkward lunch, except in passing at the supermarket.

'We had to have cold showers again

last night,' piped up Elspeth, wrinkling her nose in disgust.

'Your mum still hasn't got the hang of the old water heater then?' He chuckled.

'It's no laughing matter, Mr Taggart!' Hannah said severely, her small elfin face sharply serious. 'The fire keeps going out. It's driving Mum wild. She even said a rude word and Mum never swears.'

'I know why the fire doesn't work,' said Elspeth. 'Mum's been burning chips on it. Even I know you can't light a fire with chips.'

'They're wood chips, silly,' said Hannah in a disgusted voice. 'Not fish-n-chip type chips. Honestly, Ellie, you are stupid.'

'No I'm not. And you mustn't call me that! It's Bess now, remember?'

Hannah blushed a painful beetroot red. 'Sure.' She yanked her sister by the arm and began to run. 'Come on, slow-coach, or we'll miss the bus. Bye, Mr Taggart.'

Sam watched them go. Thoughtfully

he turned his gaze towards the Carlsons' house. There were plenty of rumours swirling around town about the Carlson family. People were speculating because they couldn't find out anything concrete about them, except that they were from England, which had been easy to work out. No way could they disguise those cute pommy accents.

As for anything else, Ria had been tight-lipped and terse, not letting any personal details slip when he'd occasionally tried to engage her in conversation in the supermarket or outside the butchers. If pushed, she scuttled away, eyes more wild and fearful than a startled rabbit's in headlights. You could almost see her sporting a little cotton-tail that flashed danger at the slightest provocation.

He'd noticed that sometimes she didn't respond when someone called her name in the street and then she would tense up, surprised, her face full of confusion.

Then this morning, with Annie calling Bess Ellie. It hadn't been the first time, but little Bess's response was telling. So it looked as though they had taken on new names. Were they hiding because they were victims of domestic violence or something along those lines? That would explain a lot. Especially Ria's hyped fragility and nervous habit of looking over her shoulder.

Perhaps it was time Sam paid her another visit. He'd kept his distance as it was obvious she didn't want company, but it went against his principles to let a lone woman struggle. He'd watched his own mother suffer until he'd been old enough — and angry enough — to stand up for her and throw out his step-dad.

Sam decided he'd call by and see if Ria needed anything. Heck, there was no harm in offering. In fact, he'd show her how to work the old chip water heater. That would be a good way to strike up some conversation and maybe discover what was actually going on.

He bowled along the rough, potholed driveway to the house and parked his ute next to her low-sprung Holden.

The place was quiet. On a makeshift washing-line, strung between a pair of gnarled apple and apricot trees, hung a handful of T-shirts and underwear that barely moved in the torpid morning breeze.

On a dilapidated wicker verandah chair snoozed a big orange cat. Sam recognised it as the feral that regularly raided his sheds for vermin and stole his dog's food when Derek, the old blue heeler, was napping.

'Found a home then, you old rogue,' he said to the cat, scratching it behind its ear. The cat stretched its legs and rolled on its back, inviting Sam to stroke his velvety soft underbelly. Sam obligingly ran his hand over the creamy, orange-tinted fur. The cat responded by snagging him with his claws.

'Not so fast, mate,' said Sam with a laugh, abandoning the ungrateful creature. 'Keep your claws to yourself while I'll go check if the lady of the house has sheathed hers.'

He knocked on the fly-screen door.

There was no answer.

'Mrs Carlson?' He heard the thump, thump, thump of kindling being chopped in the back laundry. He followed the sound and found Ria hunkered down by a battered wood heater. She had a small axe in one hand and a handful of wood chips in the other. Black smoke belched from of the firebox.

'Mrs Carlson . . . ?'

Belle sprang to her feet and spun around in one fluid motion, dropping the kindling all over the floor with a clatter. The axe swung high and curved down in a sweeping arc. Sam reared back, smacking himself broadside against the back wall and yelling at the top of his voice. The axe narrowly missed him, embedding itself in the laundry cupboard and splintering the plywood.

They stared at the axe in a static, reverberating silence. It was a toss up which one of them was the most shocked. Then Belle slumped forward and said something rude.

'I'm sorry,' she said, her voice reedy

high and shaky. 'But you scared the flipping life out of me.' She half-heartedly tried to dislodge the embedded axe.

'No kidding,' said Sam, his own voice a tad reedy and wobbly too.

He pulled off his hat and ran his hand through his hair and over the back of his neck. So much for her sheathing her claws. His heart was racketing against his rib cage like the mad, trapped possum he'd captured in her kitchen the other week. He took a deep breath and then expelled it in a rush, shoving his hat back in place.

'I think the feeling's mutual. You really had me going there for a second.' He was disgusted to hear his own voice still quivering like a wussy schoolgirl's.

'To be fair, it was your fault.' Belle took a step backwards and wrapped her arms around her torso in a defensive gesture.

'And how did you work that out?'

'You shouldn't have sneaked up on me.'

'Hey, lady, I did knock and call out!'

'Well, I didn't hear you.'

'No kidding,' he said again, his voice a little more steady now. Not so girlie high. Not so pathetic. 'I'll yell louder next time.' If there was a next time. He'd sure think carefully before making another unscheduled visit.

Belle reached again for the axe and pulled, but the blade had sunk deep, witness to the amount of force she'd put behind it. Sam was mighty glad she'd missed!

'Damn axe,' she said.'It's stuck fast.'

'Oh dear.' He didn't sound sympathetic. He didn't want her loose with the axe again.

She tried to wiggle it free.

'Here, let me.' He yanked and see-sawed the axe out of the wooden cabinet, but instead of giving it back to the woman, he put it behind him. He wasn't taking any chances.

He noted Ria, who was unnaturally pale at the best of times, was as white as her close-fitting T-shirt. She wasn't wearing her glasses so her tawny eyes were naked and exposed. And they were red-rimmed and sore. From crying or lack of sleep? And did he want to know? Did he care? Should he rethink yet again about having any involvement with this prickly young woman?

She stooped and collected up the scattered kindling, her hands shaking badly so that she kept mishandling the sticks, dropping some on the floor.

'Are you OK? Do you need to sit down?'

'I'm fine.' Mirroring his earlier action, she dragged her hand through her cropped, bleached hair, making it spike. It wasn't a good look, in Sam's opinion. He preferred long hair on a woman, feminine, soft and flowing, not this boy punk, in-your-face stuff. And he preferred women warm and fun with curves in the right places. A good armful of woman was a fine thing for a man.

Ria Carlson bombed out on all fronts. She was pencil-thin and bony. In her khaki shorts and sneakers, with her buzz cut hair, she was androgynous and unfeminine. And cold. An iceberg had nothing on her! She froze at a glance. He'd never seen her crack a genuine, warm smile. And fun? Forget it. Having brain surgery without anaesthetic would offer more laughs.

Saying all that though, there was something about the woman that got under his skin. He was attracted to her. Which was crazy, because she was crazy. Hadn't she just tried to axe him through the skull?

Eyeing her dubiously, he said, 'I still think you should sit down for a while.'

'But I have to get this stupid fire going.'

She suddenly sounded like Bess — young and vulnerable and sad. It melted some of his tension and Sam relaxed.

'Here, I'll show you how it's done.'

She stared at him for one long taut moment. 'OK then,' she said with a shrug. 'Thanks.'

He nearly said you don't have to sound so grateful but then thought better of it. She needed his help even if she didn't want it. And the girls needed it too. Regardless of the prickles, he would help where he could.

'Watch and take note,' he said.

Her hands were balled into tense fists. She briefly raised her eyes and met his. 'OK.' But she didn't sound confident.

They squatted side by side and worked in silence as he laid the paper and kindling to form a base. He struck a match and then fed the infant fire with progressively larger sticks until it was burning fiercely.

'It's easy once you know how,' he said. 'The girls will be pleased to finally have a hot shower.'

Belle raised her head sharply. Her eyes snapped as fierce as the flame now crackling in the firebox and Sam was relieved the axe was safely behind him.

'You've spoken to my girls? When? Where?'

'This morning. Most mornings. I pass them on their way to the school bus. It's no big deal.'

He watched her jaw clench, the bone brittle under the fine translucent skin.

'Relax, Mrs Carlson. We're neighbours. It's only natural I chat to them if I see them. It would be odd if I didn't.'

'I don't like them talking to people,' she said tightly.

'So I've noticed. Why?' He decided to be blunt.

'You don't need to know.'

He gazed at her for the longest moment, noting the strained lines etching her amber brown eyes, the black rings on the pale skin, skin that shouldn't be pale at this late stage of summer. There were also smudges of soot and ash on her cheeks and forehead from her failed attempts to light the fire. She exuded an air of deep desperation. If she stretched much farther, he felt she would snap under the strain.

Something infinitesimal shifted deep inside him. Her plight touched him more deeply than he'd had thought possible a month ago. Sam almost stopped breathing. No! It couldn't be!

Quickly he blocked the thought, rejected it strongly. This woman had made it clear he should butt out of her life. And she was everything he didn't want in a woman — cranky, suspicious, skinny, dangerous. A cow separated from her calf would be easier to handle!

So why Ria Carlson? And why now? He'd been single a long time. He hadn't wanted commitment since his last girl-friend had walked off with his best mate and, as an added insult, taken his dog with her. Sam wasn't sure which one he'd missed the most; the friend or the dog. But definitely not the girlfriend. He'd been well shot of her.

That was in another life, a decade ago. Suddenly it seemed he was open again to the idea of a relationship with a woman. This woman. Hell, the thought was ter-rifying!

'OK,' he said, suddenly wanting to put as much distance between them as possible.

She flicked him a suspicious glance.

'You're right,' he carried on. 'I don't need to know. It's none of my business.' He rose to his feet. 'I'd best be off. I've a load of work to do.' He was acutely aware he was gabbling but he had to get out of there.

'Thanks for lighting the fire.'

'You're welcome.'

He didn't want to let on that another fire kind of had been inadvertently lit. Because he wasn't going to feed it. It would die through suffocation and neglect. He'd make sure of it.

As Sam strode towards the laundry door, he glanced over his shoulder. Ria had her back to him by the laundry sink. Her head bowed as she turned on the taps to wash away the sooty grime. Was it his imagination, or were her shoulders shaking slightly? Was she crying?

Sam hesitated. Should he go back back inside, to put his arms around her, to comfort her?

No! Self-preservation kicked in. If he got involved with this complicated, thorny woman then where would he be? Anyway, as the lady said, her troubles were none of his business.

6

Breakfast ended up down the toilet. Again. Fifth day in a row. Belle wretched and heaved until her stomach felt it had turned inside out. This was the pits. She'd lost track of her periods over the past few weeks. Had she missed one or two? She'd put down her erratic cycle to stress. It had been an awful couple of months.

However this vomiting had nothing to do with stress. This was in-your-face, no-nonsense, common-or-garden morning sickness. Good grief — she was pregnant!

Well, Xander had wanted another baby, He'd had the skewed logic that it was an antidote for a happy marriage. Belle hadn't wanted to have another child with him. She knew it wouldn't save their marriage. A miracle was the only thing going to do that and it hadn't been forthcoming.

It must have been on New Year's Eve, when Xander had got drunk. She shut down on the memory. She didn't want to dwell on that dreadful, demeaning night. And now here she was, an outlaw and a pregnant widow. What sort of life would this baby have? How would she cope being a single mum with three kids out here?

Hey, don't even go there, she admonished herself. One day at a time . . . and there was always the chance she could make it back home, once the dust had settled.

When there was nothing left to throw up, Belle sagged and wiped her clammy face with toilet paper. She flushed and staggered out of the toilet, blinking in the strong mid-morning sunlight.

It was then she spied Sam Taggart. Damn the man! She wished he'd make himself scarce.

He was leaning against the post-and-rail fence, tall and laconic, a modern day cowboy in his dark jeans, stock-man shirt and well-worn Akubra. She'd never met anyone like him before. He suited his environment; tough and lean and raw.

What was he doing here? Goodness, every time she turned around he seemed to be there. So much for his hermit reputation!

Yes, he apparently had one. Patty Clarke had informed her, for whatever reason, when she'd baled her up the other morning, when Belle had made what was meant to be another quick a foray into town for groceries.

It was as if Mrs Clarke thought she was interested. Well, she wasn't. Yet she'd stayed chatting to the woman for a good twenty or so minutes on the uninteresting topic of Sam Taggart, finding out things she really didn't want to know, like how he'd saved his mother from his abusive step-father, taken over the struggling farm, and helped to raise his traumatised siblings, creating a stable, happy environment for them all.

He was one lone hero, in Patty Clarke's book, and worthy of a good woman. Hell's teeth if Mrs Clarke thought that

Belle fitted that role.

Belle ignored Sam while she slipped into the laundry outhouse and washed her hands in the concrete trough. She splashed water on her face and rinsed out her mouth. It didn't make her feel any better but she waited a moment to compose herself before stepping outside to see what was going on and if he was still there. He was.

'How long have you been here?' she asked.

'Long enough to hear you throwing your guts up,' he replied.

'I must have eaten something bad.'

'Right.'

'Don't worry. It's not contagious.'

'I wasn't worried,' he said mildly.

'Good, I was just saying.'

'I'm glad we've got that sorted.' He glimmered a smile so a dimple made an appearance.

Belle didn't smile back. She wasn't feeling in a smiley mood. Hadn't really done since Xander's untimely death.

'What can I do for you today, Mr

Taggart?'

Her bluntness disconcerted him. 'I don't actually need you to do anything. I brought you over some surplus salad vegetables,' he said. 'I'm all tomato-ed out.'

'Oh,' she said, surprised. 'Thank you.'

The mention of food wasn't good. There was that nasty prickly feeling and a coldness in her stomach, a sudden sprouting of perspiration on her upper lip.

'Excuse me!' She clamped her hand over her mouth and ran back to the toilet, slamming the splintered tongue-and-groove door.

Sam blinked. OK then. She obviously wasn't feeling the best. He tactfully left her to it and collected the produce from the ute and took it into the kitchen, almost tripping over the cat that fled at his appearance. While there, Sam put on the kettle and fixed her some toast.

Five minutes later she appeared at the door, wan and wary. She leaned against the doorjamb and watched him fuss about in her kitchen.

'Here,' he said. 'Put your feet up, sip the tea and have a bite of toast. Hopefully it will make you feel better.'

She regarded the tea and toast as if it was toxic waste. 'Thanks. Maybe later.'

He wasn't going to force her. She was a mother of two. She would know the drill.

'Call me if you need me.'

'Thank you, Mr Taggart.'

'You're welcome,' he said with what she thought was a hint of a long-suffering sigh.

After he'd gone, Belle sunk down on one of the kitchen chairs. She felt like hell but she knew she should try and eat something to settle her swirling nausea. She stared at the plate of toast. The cowboy had taken the time to cut the slice into neat triangles, just like he had the other day at breakfast. She picked up one and had a tentative nibble. She sipped her tea. She nibbled and sipped until most of it was gone and she was feeling better.

She placed her hands on her belly.

There wasn't much to show because she'd lost so much weight these past few weeks, but there was a slight thickening. So what was she, then? Three, almost four months gone? She had no idea. She would have to see a doctor. But not yet. Not for another couple of months or so. It was another hurdle to jump and she wasn't in a hurry to attempt the leap.

She took a deep breath. This wouldn't do. *Get a grip, woman!* She had the washing to do and sitting her in a comatose state wasn't going to get it done. She exhaled and stood up. It was time to get moving or the chores wouldn't even get started, let alone completed.

She filled the bath and tossed in towels, bed linen and a handful of underwear. A while later she was hot and bothered, flushed and tired. Hand-washing was the pits. The sheer sodden bulk of the material was heavy and hard to manhandle. Her wrist ached and so did her back and shoulders. Her fringe was stuck to her forehead and her T-shirt was soaked through with the sudsy splash-back.

She twisted and squeezed and wrung out as much of the water as possible, dropped them into the white plastic wash-basket and then lugged them outside to hang out in the sunshine. The weight of the saturated washing proved too much. The ancient washing line gave up the ghost just as Belle pegged on the last dripping sheet.

She stared in open-mouthed disbelief. 'What?' she said. 'Really?' And her shoulders drooped. She'd have to re-wash the whole flipping lot! She hauled the sodden clothes from the dusty ground, growling under her breath, and piled them into the wash-basket.

'That's a buggar. Need a hand?' Sam Taggart was suddenly there beside her, making her jump.

'Where did you spring from?' She clutched a wet towel to her chest. 'I didn't hear your ute.'

'Probably because you were muttering loud curses at the universe.'

'Those curses were justified,' she ground out and began gathering more of the fallen garments.

Sam picked up a pair of her knickers. She snatched them away. 'I can manage, thank you.'

He picked up a sheet instead. 'These sheets are still dripping wet. Isn't your spin cycle working?'

She held out her two red-raw hands. 'Don't think you can do much with these,' she said.

He gave her a questioning look.

'I don't have a washing machine, Mr Taggart.'

It was his turn to cuss. 'For goodness sake! Why didn't you say so, you silly woman? You can use my washing machine any time you need it. Here, let's take them back to the farm. There's still a chance we can get it all washed and dried before the girls get home. Or you can take some spare sheets back instead'

She closed her eyes in a tidal wave of relief. He was a life saver. Again.

'Are you OK?' There was a worried catch to his voice, which was hardly surprising as he'd witnessed her humiliating vomiting episode.

'Yes, I'm just so relieved I don't have to wash all this again. It was damn hard work.'

'Here let me carry the basket.' He shot her a concerned look. 'I came back to see if you'd recovered from your sickness.'

She gave him a twisted smile. 'I'm fine. The toast helped. Thank you.'

'Good. You need to take care of yourself.'

She rolled her eyes. 'I'm trying to.'

At the farm, Sam showed her how to work the washing machine and left her to it while he fixed them lunch.

Before joining him in the kitchen, she ruefully looked down at her damp pale blue T-shirt and wished she'd had the sense to change. She pulled the material away from her skin. Oh well. It wasn't as if she was out to impress. But she did run her fingers through her hair to make it less of a nightmare, but it didn't work. It just fell flat. She'd have to make the best of looking like a drowned albino anorexic cat and, feeling gawky and uncomfortable, she entered the kitchen.

Sam had made them a simple lunch of fresh bread and cheese with some of his home grown tomatoes. While the washing chugged away in the background, he kept the conversation light and easy, not prying at all, and she responded, not letting on that she didn't have to pry because she knew so much more about him now, thanks to Patty Clarke.

The thought niggled that perhaps he was someone she could confide in. Was that why Mrs Clarke had given her the low down? To show her that there was someone she could safely lean on? She didn't feel confident enough. She needed to get to know him better.

The time went swiftly. As soon as the washing cycle finished, they drove back to the shearers cottage where Sam fixed the line and left her pegging the washing out to dry while he returned to his farm work.

Belle felt momentarily at peace. Maybe things were going to be OK after all. Somehow.

7

Belle needed to call her mum. She wanted to hear her voice, have some normality. But she was loathe to use her own phone in case the police could track her. Or Camelo Milo. She decided to drive to the nearest large town and call from a kiosk there, to be on the safe side.

The booth was next to a brick post office and semi shaded by a Morten Bay Fig tree. The shade was welcome but the kiosk was still suffocatingly hot. She kept the door open with her foot while she dialled and waited. The phone rang endlessly. She squeezed her eyes shut and willed for someone to pick up. She was about to cut the connection when her mother, sounding breathless, answered the call.

'Mum! Thank goodness you're there.'

'Gosh, Belle! It's so good to hear from you. It's been awful. Are you alright, sweetie? Where are you? What's happening? The police want to know where you are!'

Belle wasn't surprised the police had interviewed her family. 'So you know about Xander, then?'

'Oh yes, Belle. We do. It's terrible. So tragic. I can't even begin to think how it happened. But you must have had your reasons, darling.'

'I didn't kill him, Mum!'

'Well, of course you didn't. I thought the police were being presumptuous, saying that you did. We're right behind you, sweetie.'

Belle squeezed her eyes tight shut. She would have laughed if it wasn't so tragic. Her mother obviously thought she was capable of murdering her husband! 'Thanks for being on my side.'

'Of course I'm on your side. You're my daughter. Now tell me, what can Dad and I do to help? Do you want us to come out? We will, you know. We have a little money in the kitty we could use.'

'No!' The word exploded out of her. There was no way she wanted her parents anywhere near Milo. It was too dangerous. 'No,' she said again with less urgency. You're better staying at home. Then, if I need to, I know where to find you.'

'If you say so, dear. Probably sensible. Your father's not that robust at the moment.'

'What's wrong with him?' Panic flared in her.

'He's caught a cold. It's nothing serious, though he'd like me to think it is,' and she laughed. 'You know your father. How are the girls?'

'They're fine. Doing good.'

'Weell, we're here if you need us.'

Belle closed her eyes, trying not to cry. 'I'll ring when I can. It might not be for a while.' Her voice was unsteady. 'Love to you and Dad. Bye.'

She cut the connection and then bawled her eyes out. Once she was more composed, she left the phone box and located the library. She signed in to use the internet and stared worryingly at the screen. *Get on with it, Belle*, she admonished. She flexed her fingers and then, before she could change her mind, googled her own name.

The search result was almost instant. She clicked on the first link and her picture bounced on to the screen, confronting and scary. She scrolled down the article and read the scanty report that said she was still missing and a person of interest in her husband's murder investigation. People should contact Crime Stoppers if they had information concerning her whereabouts.

Never in a thousand years did she think she'd end up a fugitive! She felt as though everyone was staring at her, condemning her. She swiftly left the library and headed for an arcade, hoping for anonymity among the shoppers. She scanned the shops until she found one that sold phones and purchased the cheapest one. She would use that locally and keep her other one locked until things were calmer, if that was ever possible.

With the ginger tom purring loudly on one side of her and a cup of tea steaming the other, Belle shook the contents of the manilla envelope on to the kitchen table. It was finally time to count Milo's money and work out how long they could survive before she needed to find work.

There was a clatter as a silver-coloured key fell out from among banknotes on to the Formica. Pumpkin jumped on to the table and batted it with his paw. Belle pushed him away and stared at the key. She didn't recognise it from any of the ones she'd used, either in the UK or Sydney. Did it belong to Xander? Or Milo? Or whoever the money had belonged to?

Gingerly she picked up the square-headed key. She turned it over in her hand. It had a serial number engraved on it. Perhaps it was a locker key, but for where? She wondered what she should do with it and then, on a whim, wrapped it in tinfoil and shoved it to the bottom of the dripping pot. No one would look for it there and it would give her time to consider her options.

She then gave her attention to the wads of cash. She sorted it into piles, securing them with elastic bands. There was much more money than she had anticipated, but nowhere near Milo's half a million. She wondered where Xander had got it from? Well, there was no way of telling, but at least the money made things a little less desperate for her.

Pumpkin sprang back on the table. Belle pulled him into her lap and began rhythmically stroking him. As he settled down for a nap, she rested her chin on her hand and gazed out the kitchen window at the clear blue sky and golden paddocks. It was crazy but she missed the grey sky and cool drizzle of England, the country lanes, the patchwork fields and teeming hedgerows, the high street shops and cosy cafes. And, of course, she missed her family and friends. Her throat constricted. Would she ever see them again? She shook her head. It wasn't worth dwelling on the negatives. She had to be strong.

Through the blur of tears she looked down at the neat piles of notes. Because there was so much cash, it meant she could put off working for a while, but how long could she keep this pretence up? For as long as it takes, she thought bleakly, a tear rolling down her cheek. There was no clear end in sight.

She heard a noise, a slight scrape of a boot on the verandah steps. The cat leapt away and disappeared into the bedroom. Heart racing, Belle threw a tea-towel over the money and turned guiltily towards the open door.

Sam Taggart stood there, holding a sack.

'Mrs Carlson.'

'Mr Taggart.' She dragged her hand across her wet eyes.

'I'm not interrupting anything?'

'Actually, you are.'

She saw him wince at the tartness in her voice and wished she hadn't been so abrupt but it couldn't be helped. She'd seemed to have lost the art of politeness since becoming a fugitive.

Sam shrugged. 'Sorry. But I've bought you something.'

'Oh.' She was at a loss. After the axe-wielding incident she didn't think she'd see him again.

'Chickens.' His eyes rested fleetingly on the table and Belle hoped he didn't spot the hundred dollar note peeking out from the edge of the cloth. 'How about I wait for you outside?' He left before she could answer him.

Quickly, Belle scooped up the money and tossed it in the bread bin, chucking the tea towel on top. She gave a cursory brush-down of cat hair and was with him in sixty seconds flat.

'Chickens, Mr Taggart?'

'I had some spares. Thought you could do with some,' he said, adding, 'For eggs.'

'I know chickens lay eggs, Mr Taggart. I might not be a country girl but I do know that much.'

'I'm glad to hear it. The girls wanted some.'

'You've been talking to my girls again?' She couldn't keep the antagonism out of her voice.

'We're neighbours, remember?' And there was a dangerous edge to his own voice, as if she was pushing him too hard. He shrugged again. 'Probably knew you'd say no.' And he gave her a tight, challenging look. 'Right?'

'Right, because we're not set up for chickens.'

'I could get that old coop fixed up for you.' He thumbed towards the tangle of wire and wood at the back corner of the garden. 'It wouldn't take me long.'

'It might not but we don't need chickens.'

'The girls need animals. It's not natural growing up without pets.'

'There's the cat.'

'Only because he adopted you, not because you wanted him, and anyway, he's a feral and independent. It'll do the girls good to look after something that relies on them for food and water. It'll teach them about responsibility.'

She threw her hands up in exasperation. 'But we might have to leave in a hurry.'

'Why?' She gave him a steely glint. 'Oh that's right,' he said. 'It's none of my business.'

'You've got it.'

'If you have to go away, I'll come and round them up and take them back home. Deal?'

She hesitated and then caved in. 'Deal. You go and fix the coop and I'll fix us a cup of tea.'

'I'd prefer coffee.'

'I only have tea, Mr Taggart,' she said flatly. She'd axed coffee on their tight budget. If she had to suffer, he could suffer too. 'You have a problem with that?' She dared him to say otherwise.

'No, ma'am. Tea'll be just the ticket, thanks. And the name's Sam. I think we've known each other long enough to drop formalities.'

Back in the kitchen, Belle packed the notes into a plastic bag and stuck it in the freezer compartment of the fridge while the kettle boiled.

Through the kitchen window she

could see Sam working on the coop. He'd already let the chickens out of the sack. They were big red birds with floppy combs and they scratched around their wired enclosure like four bossy women at a garage sale, racing from one place to another as one of them unearthed some luscious treat. One of them reminded her of Patty Clarke.

She felt outmanoeuvred by her neighbour and it irked, but she had to admit the chickens wouldn't be a bad addition to their family life. And they'd get fresh eggs, which would be special.

Belle took the tea tray out into the garden. She put the tray on the dead grass lawn and dusted off the sun-blistered bench. As she sat and waited, waving away the irritating flies from her face, she watched Sam. He was wearing his dark green shirt with the sleeves rolled up to the elbows. Sweat darkened the shirt. The jeans were grubby and frayed but he filled them well. Lean legs and taut butt, the man was all muscle and sinew from his long days on the farm.

She glanced down at her own jeans. They were a designer brand but now unrecognisable as such. They were faded and soft from too many washes. They were getting to be a tight fit. Soon she'd have to raid the op-shop and find some bigger clothes.

She ruffled her shorn hair. How she missed her long tresses, but one day she'd grow it again. And stop bleaching it. Contrary to popular belief, since being blonde, she hadn't had any fun. Another empty myth, along with true love and happy-ever-afters, she thought wryly.

She leaned back and the bench creaked in protest. She closed her eyes against the sun's glare. It glowed fire behind her lids, and she explored the red nothingness, enjoyed the rare tranquillity and sense of calmness, hearing the comforting bang, bang, of Sam's hammer as he nailed the chicken house boards back in place.

She felt safe having him there. Like she'd felt safe sleeping in his bed. The knot of panic and fear that seemed permanently lodged in her chest loosened slightly. She sighed. She felt almost — just almost — content for a brief moment.

Belle didn't know when the hammering stopped, but gradually she became aware of silence, of having someone close to her. She snapped open her eyes, her hands flicking up in a defensive gesture.

And there was Sam, squatting by the tray.

'Sorry, Ria. I didn't mean to wake you,' he said, not looking up, his hat shading his face so she couldn't read his expression.

'I wasn't asleep.' She dropped her hands back in her lap, twisting her fingers together, feeling an idiot for her overreaction.

'Could have fooled me. You looked out for the count.' He suddenly raised his head and stared straight at her. She experienced a jolt of pure energy. She hadn't realised his eyes were so blue. They shot through her like a gas flame in midnight darkness, seeking answers, wanting truth, demanding connection.

'I ... I haven't been sleeping too well.' It was an understatement. The 3am panic attacks were a regular ordeal. Often she didn't fall asleep until dawn, only to be roused by the girls for breakfast and packed-lunch making an hour or so later.

'I won't ask you why. You'll only tell me it's none of my business.' He settled back on the straw-coloured grass, stretching out full-length on his back, his hands behind his head, his hat tipped forward, so again his face was shaded from her.

There was a silence that was tempered only by the hum of bees in the nearby peach tree.

Belle sipped her tea, acutely aware of his whipcord taut body. Through half closed eyes she studied the wiry golden chest hair that spilled above the open V of his shirt. He exuded strength and calm solidness and she envied him his uncomplicated farming life where he knew who and what he was with no hidden agendas.

She let her eyes wander down the entire length of him, ending in the scuffed leather boots.

'You're wearing odd socks,' she blurted out and then wished she hadn't. Over-stepping the mark into personal territory was a no-no. The least she knew about him the better.

Sam raised his brows. 'You noticed.'

'Well, one is bright red and the other blue. How could I not notice?'

'And there I was thinking you were giving me the once over, hoping you'd approve.'

Belle blinked. Was he teasing her? Flirting with her? She self-consciously kept her eyes fixed on her mug, con-fused, and didn't answer, because she didn't know what to say. She couldn't say that she approved of what she saw, even though she did, because he might construe it as a come-on and then that could lead to all sorts of complications that she didn't need in her life.

She inwardly sighed. It had been a

lifetime ago since she'd been single and carefree and talking to an eligible man. Now she was a pregnant widow with kids, the run from the law and being hunted by a dangerous man. She shouldn't be flirting, and definitely not with her sensible neighbour. Anyway, she didn't trust her instinct when it came to men. She'd got Xander so wrong.

She'd been eighteen when she'd married him. He'd been exciting and debonair — smooth, accomplished, handsome and charming — a businessman out to conquer the world. Or at least that's what she'd presumed. She'd been so flattered when he'd said he adored her and wanted to marry her. There had been no hesitation on her part, even though her parents weren't happy.

As the years had gone by, she'd realised he was all smoke and mirrors, and that her parents had been right to treat him with caution. Xander's grand schemes were based on thin air. His wealth belonged to the banks. He became abusive when things didn't go his way or when his many business ventures failed.

Later, she'd discovered he was having affairs. She had no idea how long they had been going on, but by then she had fallen out of love and didn't care any more. When their marriage had hit crisis point, Xander hadn't want her to leave. He'd begged her to stay. He'd applied all his charm to win her over and suggested a new life abroad.

Sometime before, he'd met Camelo Milo on a business trip. Milo had wanted to set up an exclusive financial advisory business and had offered Xander a partnership. Xander had been keen as there was plenty of room for expansion.

Belle had inadvertently discovered that the expansion involved drugs and extortion. Just when had Xander gone to the dark side? But he'd told her not to be a prude.

She frowned at the memory, unaware of Sam studying her silent, closed expression. 'I've got some grain in the back of the ute for the chooks,' he said abruptly. Belle herself tore away from the black memories. 'How much do I owe you?' 'Nothing. It's a present for the girls. I'd best be off then.'

'Do you have to go?' The words escaped before she could stop them, and she blinked startled eyes at him, surprised at her own question.

Sam held her gaze for a long moment. 'I think it best, Mrs Carlson,' he said quietly.

She ducked her head. So they were back to being formal? Well, that hadn't last long, but it was a sensible move. 'Perhaps you're right, Mr Taggart. Goodbye — and thank you.'

She watched him go, his strides long and measured over her dry, crusty lawn and wondered why she felt so deflated.

8

After Sam left, Belle stayed seated on the bench. She gazed around at the clear blue sky, at the trees and farmland, the hills and her little garden. In the weeks they'd been here she'd felt the tension gradually ease within her. In spite of her fears, there'd been no police knocking at her door and she doubted if Milo would ever find them in this bucolic backwater.

She wandered over to the peach tree and plucked one of the sun-warmed, furry-skinned fruit. She sank her teeth into its succulent sweet orange flesh. The juice dribbled down her chin and she licked her fingers. The peaches were the best she'd ever eaten; fat and juicy and warm from the sun. She should harvest them and beat the pesky parrots, bees and ants.

She took the tea tray back indoors and emptied the laundry basket, lining it with newspaper, to hold the fruit. She picked as many peaches as she could reach but it irked that she couldn't quite reach the high ones. She'd be damned if the parrots got them instead of her.

She fetched a kitchen chair and made sure it was stable before clambering on to it, filling the basket. There were still a few just out of her reach. She stood on tip-toe and levered herself upwards, finding footholds among the branches, scratching herself against the rough bark. She managed to pick two more peaches and wriggled downwards, accidentally knocking over the chair.

Damn! She tried to manoeuvre but realised she was stuck. She tried to go sideways but a sturdy branch wouldn't bend for her. She tried going the other way; still no joy. This wasn't good.

She stayed uncomfortably perched there until the girls came home. By then her legs were tingling with pins and needles and she needed the bathroom.

'What are you doing, Mum?'

'Tap dancing, what does it look like,

Han? I'm stuck! Can you set up the chair for me?'

Hannah did but Belle still couldn't reach it. Her heart sank. There was only one option, not that she was keen. She gave a deep, fed up sigh. 'OK, baby, perhaps you'd better go and find Mr Taggart and ask him if you could borrow a ladder?'

'In a spot of bother, Mrs Carlson?' said Sam fifteen minutes later. He was cool and polite and looked about as excited to be there as she was to have him.

'You could say that. Thanks for coming over, but the girls could have just brought the ladder.'

'It was easier for me to do it. Let's get you down.' He placed the stepladder close to the tree and guided her down, his hands on her waist.

'All good?' he said as she reach the ground, her legs shaking.

'Yes. Just stiff from being perched up there for so long.'

'You were stupid to go up there. You shouldn't climb things,' he said.

'Whyever not?' Did he suspect she was pregnant? Surely not!

'Because I might not be around to get you down,' he said gruffly. 'You could've hurt yourself.'

'Well, I'll be careful and I won't be climbing trees again in a hurry.'

'I'm glad to hear it.'

'Thank you for coming to my aid — again. Can I pay you in peaches?'

Sam gave her a long steady look as if he was going to ask for something else as a thank you. Belle felt the sudden rise of heat in her neck. It crept to her cheeks. This couldn't be happening.

'That would be peachy,' he said.

Was it her imagination or did he sound husky? What the hell was going on?

'Ouch. That's bad,' she said breaking the sudden tension. 'While you're here, you should show the girls your present.'

'You've got us a present?' said Elspeth and gave a high squeal of excitement.

Sam winced at the sound. 'Quit that hullabaloo, little one, or you'll scare them as well as me!'

115

'What? Who will I scare?' said Elspeth.

'Come with me and I'll show you.'

The girls danced around him as they moved towards the newly fixed coop.

'Tell them how to care for them too,' Belle shouted after them. She watched her girls skipping either side of the tall cowboy. It didn't do much to quieten her heart rate. Goodness, that had come like a bolt out of the blue!

Sam left, with a big bag of peaches, as soon as he'd instructed the girls on how to care for the hens. Belle decided his quick departure was a good thing, but it didn't stop her feeling disappointed all the same.

* * *

A fortnight on and Belle ruffled the heart-shaped leaves, searching for the fat bunches of string beans in Sam's vegetable garden. The beans had grown rampantly, twisting and climbing the bamboo structure, and she mined through the lush growth, plucking the firm green fingers and tossing them into her bucket.

The Murray Grey cows were lowing, deep and long, as Sam fed them hay in the neighbouring paddock. Green parrots squawked in the pear trees as they chewed on the half-ripe fruit. Wagtails chittered with strident attitude while the magpies fluted as they looked for grubs to feed their juvenile young. There was the smell of freshly damp soil and wet grass from the morning's watering and the earthy kiss of early sunshine spiced with honeysuckle.

Belle momentarily stopped her picking to enjoy the tranquillity. The events of the past few weeks were a world away from this rustic scene. It was as if that terrible day had never happened.

If only. Poor Xander. He'd have scorned this slow, laidback lifestyle. He would have hated being pinned down to regular chores, like feeding Pumpkin and the chickens, and harvesting the garden produce. He'd always conveniently claimed he was allergic to cats when they'd asked to have one, and chickens would have been a definite no-no. He considered gardening a waste of time. He'd resisted all suggestions that life in the country would be more family friendly. He'd wanted the excitement of the city, not the gentle responsibility and rhythm of the country.

This was a safe and healing place, mused Belle. A balm to the soul. The girls were benefiting. They were less troubled and a lot more relaxed and carefree. They tumbled on the apology for a lawn, doing cartwheels and handstands, playing leap-frog. And they laughed, oh did they laugh! Such a beautiful sound after their strained, painful, confused silences of those first few awful weeks.

Then there was Sam. He'd been so good to them, in spite of her initial unfriendly attitude. He'd respected her reticence to share confidences. He helped where he could without expecting anything back. He was always there for them regardless. He was just so nice.

Nice? Well, that didn't nearly do him

justice, but she was loathe to think of a better description. Keeping him at 'nice' was good enough. She didn't want to step beyond that safe mark but she did feel she should to show her appreciation. But how? She should do something that couldn't be misconstrued. How about a cake? Yes, she would bake him a cake as a thank you. That would be a good thing to do. She'd make it after lunch and leave it in his kitchen for his afternoon tea.

★ ★ ★

The cake sat warm and aromatic in the middle of Sam's kitchen table.

Cake in his kitchen was not a good sign.

Sam scratched the back of his head, thinking. He'd had a shed-load of home-baked goodies given to him over the years. They'd been left by certain women from the town who'd wanted to bake him a lot more than just cake. But they'd eased up a while back as they'd got the message loud and clear that he wasn't looking for a wife.

So who'd left cake this time?

Of course, it could be from his prickly neighbour. His mouth tugged a smile. He didn't think she would have the same motive as those other women. She was being kind, thoughtful. It was just a cake with no hidden nuances.

He saw a note tucked under the plate and unfolded it.

Sam, Thank you for everything, the Carlsons.

That was it? Not even a token kiss? Oh well, he'd been right, then. She'd had no ulterior motive. He ignored the twinge of disappointment and instead, cut a hefty slice of cake.

★   ★   ★

It was Sam's turn to host the regular poker night. He had the remains of the cake out on the counter with snacks in case anyone was hungry.

Al Tonkin, his police sergeant mate, spotted the sponge and guffawed. 'So

120

which of our illustrious Mooralup ladies is targeting you this time, Sam?'

'Never you mind,' said Sam and kicked himself for putting out the cake. The single women's cake-giving had been a long running source of amusement among Sam's friends. He should have known his mates would josh him.

'Aw, go on! Who's got you in their spotties this time, Taggart?' said Luke, a farmer from the other side of town.

'Surely you've been through the whole town by now. Are you going for a replay? I reckon it's Barbara,' said Paul who ran the newsagents opposite the hair salon and knew her reputation.

'Or Ruth from the supermarket,' said Al.

'Sharlene from the roadhouse,' added Luke.

'You're all way off,' said Sam with a laugh. 'This was from a neighbour. As a thank you for fixing her chicken coop.' Along with a long list of other things.

'A neighbour, eh?' said Al and looked thoughtful. 'A new one?'

'Our poker nights are doomed,' said Luke.

Sam shuffled the cards. 'Don't be daft. Let's get on with the game.'

9

A few days later Sam Taggart and Al Tonkin were talking outside the post office when Ria Carlson drove past and parked a little further up the street.

'That is one weird chick,' commented Al.

'Which one?' Though Sam knew exactly who Al was referring to as he was blatantly following Ria's progress as she slammed the car door and ducked into the supermarket clutching a couple of hessian shopping bags.

Sam looked on appreciatively. She was in those old jeans of hers that a few weeks ago had been baggy and unflattering but now were a snug fit, showing off the lush curve of her bottom. The pale blue T-shirt hugged her breasts. She'd changed significantly from the skinny woman who'd arrived in town with scared eyes and pinched cheeks into a warm, round attractive lady.

The residual fear was still there, lurking in her large amber eyes, hidden behind those crazy dark-framed spectacles of hers, but it wasn't as palpable. She wasn't as secretive. Sam mused that her glasses made her look so different. They dominated her small, pixie-shaped face, masking the fine features and expressive eyes.

'Ria Carlson. Your new neighbour,' said Al. 'The cake giver.'

'Why's she weird?'

'My wife's helping out with the primary school play, doing the costumes, and she said that one of the Carlson kids offered a whole heap of wigs for the dress-ups.'

'Why is that odd?'

'These guys don't appear to have a bean between them. If that's the case, why would they have a stack of wigs? It begs some interesting questions, Sam.'

'Such as?'

'Wigs are used for disguises, mate. Work it out for yourself. I think I might do some digging on our mysterious Mrs

Carlson.'

Sam thought back on his encounters with Ria. He knew she was hiding something but was it any of their business?

'Leave her in peace, Al. She's not doing any harm.' The axe incident flashed in his brain, but he dismissed it. He'd caught her unawares, that was all. It could have happened to anyone. Except no one he'd surprised had ever thrown an axe at him before.

'I tell you, there's something fishy about her.'

'Perhaps the poor woman has had chemo or something? I know my aunt had several wigs when she was going through her cancer treatment.' It was a lame excuse. He wasn't convinced himself.

'Maybe,' said Al. 'Though that doesn't explain why she doesn't have a bank account or a Post Office box number.'

'How do you know that?' he said in surprise.

'Because I checked, mate. It's my job to protect the community. If I think

125

something or someone isn't quite right, I investigate. It's what makes me a good cop.'

Sam shoved his hands deep within his jeans pockets and rocked back and forth on the balls of his feet, feeling strangely uncomfortable. Yes, not having a bank account or postal address was odd. When he'd surprised Ria in her kitchen, he'd seen a whole heap of money on the table. Perhaps Al had a point. Maybe she was a bank robber on the run.

With two kids? Yeah, right!

He thought again about her glasses and how they made such a difference to her appearance. If she put a wig on, along with the specs, she'd look like a completely different woman.

Which made him feel even more uncomfortable. But surely she wasn't dangerous? And then the axe incident flashed in his brain again. Oh boy. Things didn't look good for that woman.

'You mark my words, mate,' said Al. 'Ria Carlson's trouble. I can smell it a mile off. My cop's antenna is twitching.'

'Well, I reckon she's a nice woman,' said Sam, deciding to stick his neck out and defend her, despite his grave doubts.

'Fancy her, do you?'

'No!' *Yes. Maybe. Yes!* 'She seems harmless.'

'Looks can be deceiving. I'd keep well clear if I were you.' Al whistled through his teeth. 'I reckon she's damn dangerous.'

Sam knew she was dangerous. She'd embedded that axe helluva deep!

Al clapped him on the back. 'You be careful, mate,' he said as he walked away. 'If you get caught up with that chick you're going to end up in deep manure. Which means no more accepting freshly baked cakes, however delicious.'

★ ★ ★

There were times when deep manure looked mighty inviting, Sam decided with a wry grin as he drove towards the Carlson household a few days later. He'd tried to take Al's advice on board, but that woman just did something to him. She'd slipped under his guard and wormed her way into his psyche so that he wanted to see her all the time. Wanted to care for her, protect her, take away the worry etching that small sweet face.

Anyway, it was Sunday, the day of rest and recreation. It was going to be another scorcher so it wouldn't hurt to ask the Carlson family to join him for a swim at the dam. Years ago his dad had planted willows on its banks to give shade. The trees were fully mature now and fringed the dam with cool green. His dad had also built a small jetty for diving and fishing. It was a good place to hang out on a hot day.

At the Carlsons' house, Sam issued his invitation. Ria was wary. The girls were ecstatic.

'Can we, Mum? Please?' begged Annie, jumping up and down on the spot. 'It'll be so much fun!'

'I've already cobbled together a picnic,' said Sam. 'I've pumped up an old inner tractor tyre for the girls to play on in the water and I've a chilled bottle of elderflower wine in the esky.'

'So this isn't a spontaneous invite?' said Belle with a reluctant smile.

'No,' he confessed. 'But I don't usually have company when I go to the dam. I thought this would make it special.'

'Then how can we refuse?'

'Just bring your bathers and towels. I've everything else we need.'

As the Carlsons scrambled around for their things, Sam waited for them in the kitchen. The black-framed glasses were carelessly tossed on the counter with Belle's car keys. Now was an ideal opportunity to check them out. Except that the cat sat there, staring disdainfully at him, as if it knew what Sam was about. It was disconcerting, but he told himself not to be daft, it was just a free-loading mog.

He shot a nervous glance towards the kitchen door. Nobody was coming. He caught the cat's eye again. Was it his imagination or was it curling its lip? Was it going to pounce? Pah, He could take it on if need be. He moved quickly and snatched up the glasses and looked through the lenses. Nothing was magnified or distorted. The lenses were plain glass. Sam pursed his lips in a silent whistle. Well, that changed things. Perhaps Al was right after all!

Sam replaced the glasses just as Ria returned to the room. The cat yowled and shot out the room, brushing past Sam's leg.

'OK, we're ready,' she said with a tight, shy smile. 'Shall we go?'

He drove them in his ute, the girls and his old blue heeler in the tray top and Ria by his side in the cab. They rumbled and bumped across the yellow paddocks to the waterhole.

'This is so beautiful,' said Belle gazing at the willow fronds skimming the water along with the iridescent blue and red dragonflies. 'You must come here a lot.'

'Occasionally, but not enough. I tend to get caught up with work.'

Sam shook out a rug and laid it out under the willows. Side by side, he and

Belle set out the picnic while the girls jumped into the water, squealing at its coolness.

'Wine?' And he held up the condensation-beaded bottle. 'It's the best the supermarket had to offer.'

Belle shook her head. 'Not for me, thanks.'

He hesitated. 'It's non-alcoholic.'

'Oh.' She shot him a suspicious glance. 'In that case, thank you.' He poured her half a glass and she set it down on the grass. Leaning back on the tartan rug, she gazed up at the bold blue sky through the willow leaves and watched the swallows swooping and soaring as they feasted on insects. 'This is so unexpected. I had no idea you had this oasis on your farm.'

'There's a lot of things you don't know about me,' said Sam, lying on his side, leaning on his elbow, watching her. 'Just as there's a lot of things I don't know about you.'

Belle stilled. 'Meaning?' There was no hiding the sudden frostiness in her voice.

'You're a bit of a mystery, that's all. People are talking,' he said, trying to keep his tone light.

'The whole of the town seem to take an inordinate amount of interest in us. I don't know why.' She snapped upright, hugging her knees, staring out across the dam where the girls were splashing and shouting at the top of their voices.

'People are curious. It's natural. We're a tight community here. People care about who and what is going on.'

'We should have stayed in a city. Nobody would have cared about us there.'

A city? Any city? Not a particular place? But he let it go. It could have been a slip of the tongue.

'Which would have been a shame. Look at Bess and Annie. It's the happiest I've seen them. Would they be this happy in a poky city rental?'

'Probably not,' she conceded. 'They love it here. But it doesn't make it any easier. They want to get involved in things like the repertory theatre and sport. But

I can't allow that.'

'I suppose you have your reasons.' Sam took a deep breath and plunged on, expecting her to rebuff him. 'Is it your husband? Is he violent?'

Belle's lips twisted in a bitter smile. 'He's dead, Sam.'

It was the first time she'd used his first name.

'I'm sorry.'

'Don't be. And yes, he was violent in the later years of our marriage.' She rose to her feet. 'I'm going in for a paddle.' Which effectively stopped their discussion. 'Are you swimming?' she tossed over her shoulder.

'In a bit.' He sprawled on the rug and watched her carefully pick her way along the beaten clay path to the jetty. She was wearing a loose blue checked shirt over her shorts, effectively hiding any baby bump, but Sam was convinced she was expecting. When he'd helped her down from the tree, he'd felt the thickening, and then there was vomiting. Yep, he reckoned she was pregnant, which meant her husband had died recently.

Belle sat on the planks, leaning back on her hands, and submerged her feet in the cool water.

Sam battled with himself. He was glad Ria was a widow. The thought that an irate, dangerous husband was on her tail wasn't a pleasant one. But she was running from someone. And did he really want to discover who or why?

Yes, he did want to know the reason and he wanted to learn all about her, every last thing.

Regardless of who or what Ria Carlson was, and against his better judgement, Sam knew he was falling for her and there was nothing he could do to stop the frightening free fall.

10

Belle sucked yet another jarrah splinter out of her palm. This wood-chopping lark was the pits. She renewed her hold on the big axe and brought it down with all her strength. The force sent shock waves up her arms. The main piece of wood bounced and off the block and hit her square on the shin causing her to squeak in pain. The smaller chip flew into the air and smacked her on the forehead and she squeaked again. She dropped the axe and hopped about, clutching her shin in one hand and holding her head with the other, muttering through clenched teeth.

'What the heck are you doing?'

Belle swung around, glaring ferociously under her raised arm at her neighbour. 'Believe it or not, Sam Taggart, I'm chopping firewood.'

'Why? It's still summer.'

'I needed some chips for the water heater.'

'That log is not for kindling, honey. It's too big and dense but ideal for the slow combustion stove in winter. You need the smaller stuff. Leave it and go and collect fallen twigs and small branches that you can snap with your hands.'

'Now you tell me!'

'I thought you'd realise. My bad. Now you've gone and hurt yourself. Let me have a look.'

He pulled her hand away from her forehead. Blood trickled from a deep cut that was already bruising and angrily swelling around the edges. He whistled between his teeth. 'Dammit, Ria, you could have really injured yourself.'

'In case you hadn't noticed, I have really injured myself, thank you very much!' Tears now blurred her vision. She sniffed. She didn't want to cry. Wasn't going to cry. Not in front of Sam.

'I know you're hurt, sweetheart,' he said gently, as if talking to a small child. 'But I meant badly. You could have knocked yourself out. Or worse. How's your leg?'

Belle, still sniffing through lack of a tissue, yanked up the material of her leggings. There was a marble-sized lump right on the shin bone, but thankfully the skin wasn't broken.

'Come inside the house and I'll bathe your wounds,' said Sam with a lop-sided smile. She slapped his hand away when he tried to help her walk. 'I'm not a cripple. I can make it on my own.'

'I was only trying to help.'

'I can manage perfectly,' she said half hopping.

'I'll get some ice to take down the swelling,' Sam said when they got to the kitchen, and he made towards the fridge.

'No!' Belle protested, trying to stand again. 'I don't mind the swelling.'

Sam he ignored her and opened the small freezer compartment of the fridge. In among the frozen peas and chicken pieces was a polythene bag. Even through the icy particles frosting the plastic, it was plain the bag was stuffed full of hundred and fifty dollar bills. Sam hesitated for a second before grabbing two bags of peas and shutting the door. He pressed the frozen packets against Belle's bruises.

Belle regarded him in mute expectation. Holding her breath, she waited for him to comment on her frozen money stash. But he kept focussing on her leg and didn't make eye contact.

'Aren't you going to say something?' she said after a long, long moment that stretched her nerves horribly.

'Like what?' He still kept his head down.

'Come on, you saw what was in the freezer.'

That made him lift his head. He seared her with his eyes. 'Lady, if you want to keep your cash in your freezer or under your mattress or down your A-cup bra, that's fine by me because it's none of my business.'

Her eyes wide, her voice insistent, she said, 'Please don't tell anyone.'

'Thanks for the vote of confidence.'

'I didn't mean to offend you.'

'No offence taken.'

But there was. She could tell from

the clenching of his jaw, the hardening of eyes, the coldness of his voice. If he didn't want to discuss the money, then that was great . . . but there was another issue she had with him . . .

'Why an A-cup?' she said with a grumble.

'Honey, if you're any bigger than that, then I'll eat cold tripe for a week.'

'Start eating. I'm a B-cup, though I admit I lost some weight a few weeks back.' Though why she wanted to explain to him was anybody's guess.

'I figured. You swim inside your jeans. Or you did until recently.'

'Oh.' So he'd noticed.

'So, how's your head and leg now?'

'Oh.' She shrugged, embarrassed she'd been on a different tack. 'Sore. Stupid. It irks me that I can't get the hang of wood chopping.'

'Leave it to me, then.'

'I don't want to impose, Sam. Anyway, I should be able to do it myself. I need to be capable and independent. I owe it to my girls.'

He sighed. 'Then I'll show you how so you won't kill yourself in the process.'

Half an hour later, when Sam was sure she wasn't concussed and the cut had been covered with a band-aid, they returned to the woodpile.

'Firstly, you should get a new axe,' said Sam as he critically studied the axe. 'This one is blunt and rusty. No wonder you can't cut with it.'

'It's all I've got, apart from the small one I use for kindling and that's not man enough.'

Sam remembered her little tomahawk too well. In his opinion, it was plenty man-enough in her hands. It still gave him the heebie-jeebies when he relived the moment.

'We'll use mine. It's in the back of the ute.'

A couple of minutes later, he was back with a much newer, meaner looking axe with a black and silver blade.

'Right,' he said. 'Hold it like this.' He demonstrated and then handed it to Belle. 'No, like this, Ria.' He stood close behind her. Belle could feel the brush of his shirt-front against her thin cotton T-shirt. She sucked in a breath and shuffled forward to minimise their contact, but he followed right behind, which was no good for her equilibrium. She shivered.

'Stand still and stop wiggling,' he commanded and moved his hands over hers on the axe handle. The warmth of his large, work-roughened hands wrapped around hers and she shivered again, in spite of the hotness of the day.

'You OK?' His mouth was close to her ear, his breath caressing the side of her neck. She shivered again. 'You're not feeling faint?'

'Yes. No. I'm fine.' Her voice was husky. Belle decided that his voice wasn't much better.

'Good. Now concentrate,' he said.

How could she, with Sam's strong, lean body moving against hers? For an inexplicable moment she felt like leaning into him and letting his muscular arms wrap around her, cocooning her from the world and all its troubles.

It had been so long since she'd been held. She missed the intimacy. Xander had been dead for weeks, and their marriage months before that, except for New Year's Eve and that hadn't been the sort intimacy she'd craved.

Flickers of long suppressed need licked deep, causing her to tremble. Madness! What was she thinking? She couldn't succumb to this sudden desperate urge to turn into him and hold him. It'd be too weird, too difficult, too everything. She was only just widowed, goddammit! Cross with herself, she tamped down her feelings and dragged her attention back to what Sam was saying.

'Hold it like this . . . Let its weight help you to bring it down square. Don't take your eyes off the target . . . ' With his hands over hers, he lifted the axe and then let it fall with one effortless, forceful thwack. The wood split cleanly in two. 'Like that,' he said, satisfaction ringing in his tone.

They did it again and again and again.

'Now do it on your own.' Sam stepped away.

Belle ignored her sense of disappointment, flexed her muscles and lifted the axe. She swung down . . . and missed.

'Try again, but hold your hands further apart.'

This time she hit the wood at a wonky angle and the log rolled away. 'Damn!' she said.

'Don't worry, kid. It takes practice.'

She did it again and missed.

'Hold it like this.'

Sam came back around her and repositioned her hands. Belle must have leaned back because suddenly he tensed. She felt the hardening of his body at the same instant hers began to melt.

The next moment the axe was forgotten. It fell on the ground between them and his arms were around her, cradling her into him.

'Ria,' His mouth was a breath away from her hair. 'You don't have to do this.'

Belle trembled, confused. Was he talking about the wood chopping or being in his arms? She moved slightly, perhaps trying to put distance between them, or perhaps trying to get closer? She wasn't sure which, but it felt good whichever way she looked at it.

'Let me help you,' he said, his arm tightening further, preventing her from leaving. 'And I don't just mean cutting your firewood. It's obvious you're under a lot of pressure. Let me share your burden, whatever it is.'

Belle put the heel of her hands against her eyes. This was crazy! She leaned further into him, knowing she shouldn't but not being able to help herself. It had been so long since someone had actually cared about her. She'd felt so alone for so long in her loveless marriage, and desperately isolated since fleeing Sydney. But was this sensible for either of them?

'Sam, I can't let you help me.' Her voice caught. 'Not just you — anyone.'

'Why not?

'Because I don't know who to trust.'

'Start with me, honey.'

'You don't know what you're asking.

Or what you'd be getting involved in.'

'I don't care.'

'You will and you'll live to regret it.'

He turned her gently around to face him. She stared up into his weather-browned face with his piercingly clear, sky-blue eyes and his untidy thick blond hair and she wished things could have been different. But there was the shadow of her murdered husband. And the reality of Camelo Milo who was out there, intent on hunting her down. To top it all off, she was wanted by the police!

One of Sam's hands dropped to the swell of her hip, the other cupped the back of her head.

'I doubt it,' he said, and leaned towards her so that his lips were a bare millimetre away from hers. As his sun-warmed lips met hers, Belle felt the ground tilt. Her hands went up to clutch his shoulders and Sam deepened the kiss.

As far as kisses went, it was relatively chaste though full of promise. She could feel the banked passion ready to flare at the slightest provocation. But did she want to provoke it? And did he?

Sam broke the kiss. 'So, tell me what's wrong, Ria.' He said, his voice endearingly uneven.

'I can't.' She bit her bottom lip, her eyes downcast, her fingers nervously fiddling with Sam's shirt button, totally unaware of the effect she was having on him, too busy with her own troubled thoughts.

'Like they say in the movies, it's a long story.'

'You already told me it's not your husband who's after you, so who's put this fear into you?'

Belle shivered and Sam held her closer. He smelled of tractor grease and eucalyptus leaves and sweat. A lifetime ago she wouldn't have found those scents appealing but now they were an aphrodisiac and a comfort rolled into one.

'It's complicated . . . dangerous . . .'

She leaned her forehead against his chest and breathed in his smell again. She couldn't help it. She was already addicted. Sam ran his fingers through her silky, spiky hair and then gently tugged on it so that she tipped her head back and looked straight into his eyes.

'I don't care how complicated it is. I get that you're hiding from someone.'

'It's that obvious?'

'To me, yes.' And maybe most of the town, but he didn't think she needed to hear that.

'I can't talk about it, Sam. It won't change anything if I tell you.'

'It might help. I'm here for you, Ria.' And then he kissed her again. And this time it wasn't so chaste. Not by a long shot. It was deep and hot and all-consuming and Belle sunk into that kiss, revelling in its bone melting heat. Passion encompassed her. Drawing her down into a vortex of pounding blood and surging adrenaline.

Then her damn conscience began beating a tattoo in the middle of her brain, telling her this was one of the stupidest things she could do given the circumstances. The voice of reason dragged her back from paradise, back to cold reality.

The kiss faltered.

'This isn't a good idea, Sam.'

'I can't think of a better one, honey.' He chuckled and gathered her back into his body but Belle pushed against his chest, feeling the heady, rapid beat of his heart beneath her open palm.

She levered herself away from him. 'No! I can't. I'm so sorry. I wish it could be different but there's no way we can be together.'

Blindly, stumbling over the uneven ground, she ran towards the house. She wrenched open the back door and ran into the cool, dim house. The fly-screen door slammed behind her. She flung herself on the old double bed. It creaked protestingly as she burrowed under the pillows and quilt, trying to block out what had just happened, wishing she hadn't been so stupid, berating herself for giving into temptation and kissing Sam. Yet so pleased that she had!

After a while, Belle padded barefoot to the back door and peeked through the fly-screen mesh. She'd expected Sam to have left, but there he was, wielding his axe with pure masculine grace and strength and perfect rhythm. She supposed it was one way of dealing with frustration and she grudgingly envied him his release.

Sam must have felt the prickle of her gaze. He suddenly straightened and turned in her direction. He tipped back his hat and swiped at the sweat on his brow while he stared straight back at her.

The next moment, he chucked the axe to one side. It fell with a clatter against the pile of logs. He strode over to the cottage and swung open the door. Belle didn't move. She should have, but she didn't.

Sam strode into the room and took her by the shoulders, dipped his head and claimed her lips in one hard, swift kiss.

He broke away and looked deep into her wide tawny eyes.

'This isn't over,' he said. 'I'm sticking by you and the girls, and helping you with whatever this thing is that's eating you up and causing you to run scared. You need me, Ria.'

He kissed her slightly parted lips again with masculine certainty.

'And I need you for a whole load more reasons.'

Then he spun round and left!

Belle hungrily watched his departing figure. She lifted her fingers to her lips, lips that were tingling and alive from his kiss.

She been living in a vacuum of fear but Sam had changed that. He was like a breath of pure oxygen. He was her sanctuary. But only if she had the courage to let him into her sorry life.

11

Hannah and Elspeth waved to him as they dog-trotted towards the bus stop the following morning. 'Hi, Mr Taggart!'

'Hi, girls. Have a good day at school,' he called back. He then turned his head in the direction of the cottage. There was that constant, insistent pull to go and see Ria Carlson.

Not only see her, but kiss her senseless! What had got into him? He was as fixated as a teenage boy with his first crush! He had work to do; he shouldn't be mooning over a woman.

But why fight it? He quirked a smile. Why indeed. He wasted no more time and drove over to the cottage.

He parked under the oak. Autumn wasn't far off. The tree was shedding its acorns. The green bullets crunched under foot as he strode to the front door. There was no reply. He wandered down the broken concrete path along the side of the house and into the back garden.

* * *

With Pumpkin weaving between her legs, purring like a jet engine, Belle was under the nectarine tree, checking for ripened fruit. She reached through the leaves and clasped her hand around a smooth, firm nectarine. She placed it a cardboard box and reached for another. Several nectarines later she felt a burning on her legs. She glanced down. Big black ants were swarming up her jeans.

She squealed, scaring the cat, and bounced backwards, hitting her head on one of the low slung branches and up-ending the fruit. She squealed again as the ants swarmed further up her jeans. She swatted at them but could feel them biting her flesh.

She grappled with her boots, flinging them away, she wrenched down the zip of her jeans, shucking them at breathneck speed and throwing them after the boots, slapping at her legs, brushing away the biting ants, hopping around on the parched ground.

'Jeepers,' said an amused voice from the other side of the tree. 'I wasn't expecting that sort of entertainment today. Not that I'm complaining.'

'Hah!' She prised off another ant that had sunk its teeth into her socks. It was then she realised how daft she must look in her daggy T-shirt, underpants and socks. 'Don't look!'

'Too late.'

'A gentleman would turn his back.'

'I've never claimed to be one . . . OK, OK, I'll shut my eyes.' He did but there was still a big grin on his face. 'But only for a moment,' he warned with a rumbling laugh.

Belle couldn't help but smile too. It was a good job his eyes were closed. She didn't want him to see she was responding to him. Things were already awkward between them, especially after yesterday's kisses.

While he stood there smirking, she shook out her jeans and pulled them back on fast.

'I'm decent now,' she said.

'Shame.'

His blue eyes sought hers and she felt her breath leave her body, the smile die on her lips, the heat rise in her cheeks.

'Sam. About yesterday . . . It shouldn't have happened.'

'But it did,' he said matter-of-factly.

'Yes, but . . .'

'And it was good.'

'Yes, but . . .'

'So you agree it was good?'

'Yes, but . . .'

'No buts. Let's do it again.'

He held his arms wide open, inviting her to step into his embrace, his eyes hungrily holding hers, willing her to close the distance between them.

She held her hands against her cheeks. 'No!' She shook her head. 'It would be disastrous!'

'Maybe for you, but not me.'

'Sam, it's madness. There's no future.'

His arms dropped to his sides. 'So what? That's life. I'm willing to take the gamble.'

'You don't understand,' she whispered, her fingers over her mouth, holding back any emotion.

'Only because you won't share your problems with me so that I can understand. But I want to understand, Ria.' He took a step closer. 'You see, all I know is that it was so damn good having you in my arms.' And he held them up again, another invitation to be held close. 'And I want you back there. Come to me, Ria.'

She closed her eyes, vividly remembering his strong hold, his sure lips. 'No.' It came out more of a breathless sigh than a word.

'This thing between us isn't going to go away any time soon, honey. You do realise that?'

'But, Sam . . .'

'Look, I came on too strong. I apologise.'

'Don't apologise.' And she couldn't help the sudden upward tilt of her lips.

He grinned. 'OK, I won't.' He took another step closer to her and reached out to cup her cheek in his large work roughened hand. 'Here's the deal, Ria. We take it nice and slow — or I'll try to. I won't push — or try not to — and we'll see where it takes us. How about it, kid?'

'That's a bad, bad idea, Sam Taggart.'

'It's the only one I've got. I'm not a man who needs a woman in my life so I'm not planning on cramping your style. Let's just enjoy each other and see what happens.'

'I'll think about it,' she hedged, though her heart was swelling at the sheer wonder that he wanted her. 'But no promises.'

'Good. Let me know when you're ready. Because it's going to happen.'

'I might not say yes, Sam.'

'You might and that's what I'm banking on.'

'You could live to regret it.'

'I don't believe in regrets. Take a chance, Ria. It'll be so good between us.'

'You're crazy.'

'Crazy for you.'

His smile took her breath away. She closed her eyes, savouring the amazing feeling of being wanted, cherished, desired.

His lips found hers in a gentle kiss and she snapped open her eyes and stared straight into his striking blueness. The heat was there, banked and waiting. Her eyes fluttered shut and she moved into the deepening kiss with happy, inevitable acceptance.

★ ★ ★

I'm not a man who needs a woman in my life.

Really?

Sam shook his head as he drove home later from Ria Carlson's cottage, thinking about his words. Boy, he should have been a politician because who was he kidding? Didn't need Ria? He wanted that woman in his life, in his home, in his bed, because she sure as hell was already knocking loudly on his heart.

He felt buoyant. Alive. Exhilarated. Life was about to get interesting. He'd never expected to meet the right woman and here she was, right next door to him. Who'd have thought?

* ★ *

'Wasn't it exciting seeing the kiddies on TV,' said the woman at the check-out.

Belle stared at her blankly. 'The kids?'

'Last night. On the regional news.'

'Were they?' Belle said, filling up a cardboard box with groceries and taking out her purse. She had no idea what was the woman going on about.

'It was the primary school's play. It got selected to go through to the state final. SW TV did a piece on it. You didn't see it? What a pity.'

'We don't have a TV,' she managed to stutter while her blood ran cold. The kids were on TV?

'Oh, what a shame. You'll have to find someone who's recorded it. It's well-worth seeing. The kiddies were so cute, especially your little Bess.'

Belle left the supermarket in a daze. The girls on television? No! It couldn't

158

have happened! Surely the school would have asked parents for their permission? Oh heavens, what if someone saw it and passed on the information to Milo? It didn't bear thinking about!

When the girls came home from school, Belle was waiting for them at the bus stop. She was tight-lipped and abrupt.

'What's wrong, Mum?' Hannah asked as they walked down the farm track towards the house.

'A lot,' she said uncompromisingly. 'Did you know you were going to be on TV last night?' Belle tried to sound calm but she could feel the coils of tension curling into tight knots in her stomach, causing her voice to come out hard and stilted as she battened down the volcanic rush of anger.

The girls didn't answer, bowing their heads, hiding their faces so she couldn't read their expressions, but their guilt radiated from them like a forcefield.

'So I'll take that as a yes, then.'

There was silence except the crunch,

crunch, crunch of gravel under their shoes.

'Why didn't you tell me?'

'You knew about the play,' said Hannah defensively.

Belle stopped abruptly and confronted her girls, her hands on her hips, frowning. 'And I had no problem with that. I was looking forward to seeing you both on stage on Friday. It's the TV appearance I'm concerned about. Don't you understand why' She flung her hand in the air.

'If we had told you we were going to be filmed you would have stopped us,' said Hannah, lifting her chin defiantly. 'And we had big parts. We would have let the others down if you'd said we couldn't be in it after all those rehearsals. There weren't any good understudies to take our roles.'

'It was my call to make whether or not you could be filmed. How come I didn't get a letter from school telling me about it?'

The girls stared at her wide eyed and

pale.

'This is your fault,' said Elspeth to Hannah and she began to cry.

Hannah's face flushed bright red. 'They sent you a letter. And a form,' she admitted.

Belle was trying very hard to keep a handle on her temper. She'd worked so hard to find them a safe haven only for the girls to jeopardise it.

'I hid the letter and filled in the form for you,' she whispered.

'Oh, Hannah!' said Belle, the words wrenched from her heart. 'What have you done?'

'I know I shouldn't have forged your signature, Mum, but it's no big deal. You're always faking things now. And we couldn't leave the others in the lurch. And,' she sniffed, 'we looked great on telly. Our teacher showed us today.'

'I'm sure you looked wonderful but because of that we'll have to pack and leave,' said Belle, fear and anger tumultuously warring for supremacy.

'No, Mummy!' said Elspeth crying

harder. 'I like it here. I don't want to go!'

'Nor me,' said Hannah trying her best not to cry like her sister.

'You should have thought about that before you lied to me,' said Belle. She stalked off to unpeg the washing from the line. How could the girls have been so irresponsible? They knew it was imperative they kept a low profile.

She was so preoccupied with her grim thoughts that she didn't hear Sam's ute. Ten minutes later, when she wrestled the full basket into the kitchen, three pairs of eyes regarded her with mixed degrees of wariness.

'Sam!' She dumped the basket on a chair and began to rapidly and untidily fold the clothes.

'Ria.'

'You'll need to take your chickens home.' She smacked a T-shirt onto the table.

Sam took a deep breath. 'So it's true, then. You're going to leave? Just like that?' And what about us? Hung in the air unsaid.

Belle stared hard at the girls. Elspeth sniffed and wiped her brimming eyes. Hannah rebelliously stared back. 'I told Mr Taggart you were mad at us,' she said.

'Does he know why?' Belle responded tautly. 'And that it's your fault?'

'I think you're overreacting,' said Sam.

'Think what you like, it doesn't change anything. We're leaving.' She thumped down another T-shirt.

'If that's what you want.'

She glowered at him over the higgledy-piggledy pile of laundry. 'It's not what I want, but we have to go for our own safety! We can't risk staying here now that the girls have been on TV.' And she added a towel to the pile which unbalanced it. Sam caught the pile and re-jigged it for stability.

'It was just the local south-west channel, Ria.'

'Which also goes throughout the state.'

'Only the rural sector.'

'Someone might see it who'll recognise us.'

'I very much doubt it.'

'I don't. You don't understand what we're up against.'

'So tell me, hey?'

There was loud silence while Belle continued folding the sun-crisp clothes, making a new pile. Tears blurred her vision. 'I can't,' she finally said.

Sam growled deep in his throat and dragged his hand through his hair, making it peak. 'How about you just lay low for a week or so and see what happens?'

Belle bunched her fists in a tea towel and pulled it to her chest as if she was stemming the bleeding of her breaking heart. How could this be happening? She'd thought that perhaps she'd finally found safety with a loving, decent man but it was now over before it had even begun.

'I don't know,' she said and her voice was full of anguish. 'I don't know what I should or shouldn't do! This is all so hard.'

'Please, Mum,' said Hannah, sensing weakness. 'People won't recognise us with our different hair.'

'They might.' But Hannah had a point. The girls did look different with their short blonde pixie cuts and tanned faces.

'Please can we at least stay until the play is done? That's only three days. Please? Please!'

'I can move in if it would make you feel safer.'

Was that Belle's imagination or did a streak of red colour Sam's cheekbones? And how did she feel about having him sleeping over? She felt her own blood rise and flood her face. It wouldn't be safe at all!

'What do you say?' said Sam.

'Would you bring your gun?' she said as she returned to her manic laundry folding.

'Hell, no!'

She raised her eyes. 'Then you wouldn't be welcome, Mr Taggart.'

'Good grief, Ria. You can't think I'd need my gun? This is Mooralup.

'Mr Taggart bring your gun and keep us safe so we can stay till after our play?'

pleaded Hannah.

'If he brings the gun, then I guess so,' said Belle but with reluctance. 'But we must be ready to leave straight after the play. No arguments.'

The girls were ecstatic and flung their arms about their mum.

'Go and start packing your things,' said Belle. 'So we're well prepared.'

The girls gave her one more hug before racing out the room.

'I'm not bringing my gun,' Sam re-stated.'It's nuts to even think that I would.'

She gave him a level look. 'Shame.You should go. I've got packing to do.'

'You don't mess about, lady.'

Sam did that hair-ruffling thing again and Belle had a pang that she'd never earn the right to be able to run her fingers through its golden thickness, to ruffle it, to smooth it down. Their relationship hadn't stood a chance.

'Nope,' she said and collected up the piles of clothes in her arms and followed the girls to their room without saying goodbye. 'Life's too short.'

★ ★ ★

Belle shot upright in bed, catapulted from a deep, dreamless sleep. Her heart pounded painfully against her ribs. Her senses were on red alert. What had woken her? Then she heard panicked cackling and squawking coming from the chicken coop.

She flopped back on the bed, relief flooding through her. Damn fox was making his rounds. He'd been around a couple of times already since they'd got the hens, hoping for a free meal. She lay there for a few moments, listening and letting her heartbeat return to a more even rhythm.

The chickens sounded really spooked, their high-pitched protests reaching heady heights. Belle flung back the sheets and padded to the back door in her white T-shirt that doubled for a nightie. The night was warm so she didn't need her jacket. She stuck her feet into a pair of thongs and grabbed the broom. If foxy was out there, she'd give him what for.

The moon was only a slither off full. It bathed the backyard in soft, green-tinted hues, making it easy for Belle to find her way across the scratchy grass. She was halfway across the lawn to the hen house when it hit her. What if it wasn't a fox?

Fear washed through her. It whirpooled in her belly and flooded her limbs. She stopped and listened hard, straining to hear anything, something, above the chickens' raucous din.

That was it, the broom wouldn't be enough. She needed the axe.

She forced herself to move forward and tip-toed to the woodpile. As silently as she could, she swapped the broom for her old blunt axe. Holding it in her fear-sweaty hands, she moved stealthily towards the coop. There was a scrape of wood, a rustle of leaves and the hens increased their cackling. Belle just about stopped breathing. Getting a better grip on the axe, she raised it above her head and took a shaky step forward.

There was a bulky shadow moving between the chicken shed and the lemon-scented gum and Belle knew it was no damn fox. Adrenaline pumped through her. She re-adjusted her grip on the smooth, weathered axe handle.

There was a sudden crack of rifle shot, a flurry of feathers and Belle screamed, bringing down the axe hard and shaving off a slice of timber from the side of the weatherboard coop.

There was a barrage of foul language followed by an incredulous, shaky laugh. 'Whoa, woman! You planning on taking a chunk out of me?'

Belle sucked in a sharp breath. 'Sam Taggart, I could have killed you!' she yelled, flinging the axe on the ground and launching at the man as he stepped out of the black shadows. She pummelled him with her fists in anger and relief.

'Hey! Steady, girl, steady!' Sam tried to catch her fists but wasn't successful. One smacked him on the chin, another knocked off his hat. 'It's OK, Ria. Hush. No one's going to hurt you.'

Suddenly all the fight went out of her and she slumped against him, letting

169

him cocoon her in his strong arms. 'I thought you were Milo. I thought you'd come to kill us!' And she began to sob uncontrollably, weeks of pent-up emotion spilling out in a torrent, drenching his rough cotton shirt.

'Oh Ria, Ria, what am I going to do with you?' Sam murmured into her hair. 'Settle down, honey. It's all good now. You're fine.'

'But you shot something.'

'It was just the old dog fox out for the chooks.'

His hands were rubbing her back in comforting circles, and she was close as she could be to his lean, warm body, absorbing his reassuring strength. As her sobs subsided she became aware of how vulnerable she was, being held against him, and wearing so little. But it felt so good, so utterly right. But she was fooling herself. Of course, it wasn't right!

Determinedly, she thrust him away before either of them did something they'd live to regret.

'Did you get him?' she said, tugging at

the hem of her T-shirt. It barely covered her bottom. She glanced up warily at Sam; his eyes glinted back in the moonlight. Her own night vision was good because of the light moon, which meant his probably was too and he was getting an eyeful.

'Yup. He's over there. I'll sling him in the back of the ute and take him home to bury.'

'I'd appreciate that.'

'You'd better get back to bed, Ria. There's still enough of the night to get some shut-eye.'

'OK' She hesitated. 'Sam, what were you doing in the hen house at this time of night? And with your gun? I didn't think you were going to have it anywhere near our place?'

The moon's soft rays caught his face and she saw his features harden.

'You seemed so steamed up that you'd be under attack, I thought I'd do a bit of a security patrol. I threw the gun in just in case. Guess the old fox wasn't expecting that.'

'No. And neither was I. But thank you. I really do appreciate you taking me seriously.'

'I'm not convinced though.'

'I'm not making it up. We are in danger.'

'Whether it's real or not, it is to you, so I'll take it seriously, for your sake. Now go back to bed.'

'You should too.'

'I might stick around a little longer.'

She paused a beat. 'Do you want to do your bodyguard routine inside?'

It was his turn to hesitate. 'I think it's better I stay out here, Ria. There maybe too many distractions indoors for me to keep a vigilant watch.' The moonlight picked up his grin.

'Ha! It takes two to tango, Mr Taggart!'

His soft laughter followed her all the way back to the house. She lay in bed thinking of him out there by the chicken coop. A smile tugged at her lips as she tugged the thin cotton sheet over her bare legs. It felt good to have him close by.

It would be better to have him even closer.

She buried her head under the pillow and groaned at her own wayward imagination because, however tempting, she couldn't embroil Sam in her sordid life. He deserved so much more. He was such a decent man and she . . . ? Well, she was a woman on the run, wanted for murder.

★ ★ ★

Sam felt scratchy-eyed and cranky. Lack of sleep never sat well with him. He'd abandoned the Carlson watch just as the sun cracked over the horizon, bathing the trees and paddocks with a new-spun gold dazzle. He'd drunk a couple of strong black coffees, done some basic chores on the farm and was now in town, catching up on business before hitting his bed. The cool sheets and darkened bedroom called to him like a siren lover, but that joy would have to wait. He still had a couple of calls to make.

He thought of Ria. In his opinion, she

was overreacting about the TV show. He couldn't see why she was so uptight and fearful, though he appreciated that for her, the fear was very real and because of that, he'd volunteered to keep doing night watches so she could sleep in peace.

Whether or not she had slept was debatable. Her bedroom light was often on, a tempting beacon during his lonely night-watches. A beacon he resolutely ignored.

As Sam came out of the supermarket, carrying a couple of bulging bags of food, and looking forward to his bed, he spotted Ria. She was unloading a huge trolley-full of groceries into her station-wagon as if she was stocking up for an expedition. As if she was leaving. The idea made his stomach churn and clench. He'd hoped she'd abandoned that plan. She hadn't mentioned it again and so he'd presumed she'd shelved the idea of running. Obviously not.

'What's all this?' Sam came up behind her.

Belle jumped. 'Sam, you gave me a

fright!'

'Good job you didn't have an axe in your hand, then. Might have been third time unlucky for me.'

She gave him a look and threw in some more bags. She was wearing her big black-framed glasses again. They slipped down her nose every three seconds, and she'd shove them back up to the bridge with her forefinger. He didn't know why she bothered. They weren't much of a disguise.

'So,' he indicated the car with a wave of his hand. 'You planning on going somewhere?' In spite of his good intentions, he sounded accusing.

'You know I am. I thought I'd be organised and have everything packed and ready to go after tonight's performance in the play.'

Sam felt as though he'd been slugged in the solar plexus. 'You're still leaving? Even though nothing has happened these past few days?'

She straightened her back and gave the street a sweeping study, obviously looking for something or someone. 'You didn't expect me to change my mind, did you?'

'Yes, actually, I did.' Sam plonked down his own shopping by his feet and automatically scrutinised the street-scape too, though he didn't know what he was supposed to be looking for.

'Hey, Ria, as a matter of interest, are we looking for anything in particular?'

'Strange people, suspicious cars . . .'

He huffed, fed up. 'Dammit, woman, you really are paranoid! This is Mooralup, the most placid, boring town in the southwest. Nothing happens here. There's nothing to worry about.'

'Well, I know there is.'

'But you're not going to tell me, right?' He slung his hands on his hips and glared at her.

Belle glared right on back, pushing her glasses into place. 'Right.'

'Look, lady, I've been sitting by your hen house night after night and there hasn't been one strange incident apart from the fox, and that wasn't even strange.'

'I've appreciated your presence,' said Belle. 'You know that. But I still reckon the girls and I are in danger. I still think we should go.'

'You're going to run away on a paranoid whim? I thought you were more sensible than that.'

'This is no whim. This is a life and death.'

'And I wouldn't understand, right?'

'You'd understand it alright, but I'm not going to tell you and embroil you in our troubles.'

'You don't think I deserve some explanation?'

'I'm not telling you. You can't get involved.'

'I've been watching your back for three nights. I am involved. Dammit, Ria, I care! About you, about the kids. I damn well care.' He couldn't believe he was actually saying that out loud and in the middle of Mooralup high street. 'I want you to stay.'

Needed her to stay! Life without Ria

would be unbearably lonely. He didn't want to contemplate it. Was it his imagination or was she crying? It was difficult to tell because of those damn stupid glasses were glinting like a battle shield, hiding the woman and her emotions.

Ria turned her back on him, loading more stuff into the car. 'We're going. End of story.'

'You're blowing it out of proportion and getting yourself wound up for nothing,' he insisted.

She suddenly spun back to face him. Her hand snaked out and she grabbed his shirt-front, hauling him towards her, unbalancing him. 'Kiss me,' she said, wrapping her arms tightly around his neck. 'And don't ask questions.'

'What the — ?'

'I said don't ask questions,' and with that her mouth was hot and sweet on his.

Well, what could a man do? Only one thing under the circumstances. Sam kissed her back, pulling her closer and closer with every heartbeat.

His fingers slid through her silky hair,

which had grown longer these past few weeks. He cupped the back of her head as the kiss deepened, going on and on, Sam revelling in Ria's glorious warm softness. How could he have ever thought she wasn't his sort of woman? Because she had curves in all the right places, yes sir! And she was kissing him as though her life depended on it.

Sam relished her intensity and tightened his grip so her whole lush length was melded to his. He forgot they were standing in the middle of Mooralup high street on a busy Friday morning. Forgot every man and his dog would see them kissing in broad daylight. Forgot everything but this sweet woman melting in his arms.

Without warning, Ria suddenly unglued her lips from his and peeked over his shoulder. 'That should do it,' she said, trying to sound matter-of-fact though an unsteady huskiness betrayed her. She half-heartedly pushed Sam away.

'Huh?' Passion fuddled his brain.

What was she saying? 'What should do it?' He nuzzled her neck, smelling the sweetness of her.

'Behave yourself,' she said, giving his arm a playful slap. But her altered tone alerted him. He raised his head and stared into her wide, tawny eyes. The glint of her plain lenses didn't mask the troubled wariness there and he didn't think, for one moment, it was caused by their kiss.

'Ria?'

'The guy's gone. I've got to go. Goodbye, Sam, and . . . and thanks for everything.' She hugged him hard before releasing him.

'Goodbye? Thanks? Hang on a minute!'

This sounded horribly like one big brush off. But, hell, he wasn't going to be dismissed so easily. And especially not after that fantastic kiss they'd just shared! You couldn't just ignore something as spectacular as that.

But she was already sliding into the driver's seat of her Holden and buckling her safety belt.

'Ria!'

'Can't stop, Sam. Gotta go.'

And this time there was no mistaking the brimming moisture in her eyes. She angled her head downwards as a tear slid down her cheek.

'But Ria, this is crazy.' She was crazy! But was she listening? Heck, no! Did she ever?

Sam watched with a mixture of anger and disbelief as she drove off. So what was all that about? Surely that wasn't meant to be their final farewell, just like that? As if these last weeks had counted for nothing. No! He wouldn't allow it. Couldn't. He didn't want her to go!

There was a slow hand-clap behind him. Sam spun round.

'Hey, mate, that was some performance,' said Al Tonkin. 'Not something we see every day in our placid little town. I thought the two of you were going to combust on the spot!'

'Ditto,' said Sam, bitterness spiking his voice. His blood was still pounding around his body. Why had she broken the kiss? Why had she run off like that? What guy?

'So it's hotting up between you two?' said Al.

'We have our moments.'

'You need your brains tested, mate. She might be great in your eyes, Sam, but she's dangerous.'

Dangerous? Didn't he know it! His body was still humming from her kiss.

'Your point being?' he said.

'I'm waiting to confirm details then I'll tell you.'

'Oh come on, Al. She's no more dangerous than the next woman.' Sam snatched up his shopping bags. 'I'm off. I've things to do.'

Like getting the hell over to the cottage and take up where they'd left off and persuade Ria Carlson to stay.

★ ★ ★

Belle felt she was going crazy. She'd been so sure she'd seen Milo driving down the main street. It was something about the turn of his head, the type of car. She chugged along the street in the old Holden, searching for the car. She saw it parked outside the chemist. She drew in to a parking spot under a tree and waited, a knot of tension bang in the middle of her chest. She almost stopped breathing when a swarthy man emerged from the chemist and got in the car. Then she expelled the air. Being so close, she realised it wasn't Milo, just someone of similar build and colouring.

Her whole body relaxed. Her lips tilted in a wry smile. So she hadn't needed to snog Sam in the middle of the high street. But that had been a bonus. Shame she couldn't try it again sometime, but she and the girls would be leaving tonight, as soon as the play ended. She put the car into gear and drove sedately home.

★ ★ ★

Sam was already there, leaning against his ute with his arms folded. Belle's heart jumped in her chest at the sight of him. Her blood began to zing at the same pitch it had reached during their street kiss. 'What are you doing here?' she said.

'You are not brushing me off after that sensational kiss. What it was that all about?'

'Ah.' So he thought it was sensational, did he? Well, didn't she? Oh, yes!

'Ria? You kissed me in broad daylight, smack in the middle of town. There must have been a very good reason for such a public display?'

'I was using you for camouflage. I thought I saw the man we're hiding from. But it wasn't him,' she said sheepishly. 'I followed the car and had another look at him.'

'So you kissed me under false pretences?'

'Guess so.'

'Feel free to do so again.' He grinned.

She grinned back but shook her head. 'It's best I don't, Sam. We're leaving tonight.'

'And I will ask you — no beg you —

not to go.'

'But we have to. We're in danger.'

'Nothing has happened since the TV story was aired. Look about you. Do you really want to leave?' *Leave me?* he wanted to say.

She let her eyes rove over the house and garden, the rolling paddocks, the trees. She couldn't help but absorb the peacefulness of her surroundings. No, she didn't want to go. She didn't want to run.

'Stay.' His voice was low and husky.

The tenseness in her shoulders eased. 'OK. Maybe we will be alright.'

He closed his eyes, relaxing too, and offered a silent prayer. 'Of course you'll be alright. Let me take the shopping inside for you.'

'I can do it.'

'Let me, Ria. You're tired. You should rest before tonight. I can come to pick you all up?'

'Are you coming too?' she sounded surprised.

'Of course I'm coming! Do you think

your daughters would let me skip it?'

Belle laughed. 'I suppose not.'

'I'll be back here by six . And for the record, if you see anyone suspicious, feel free to kiss me!'

* * *

At the school, amid the noisy bustle of people arriving to watch their children, Ria kept her head down and chose their seats at the back of the hall, close to the exit.

'You don't want to go up front for a better view?' said Sam. 'There are some places free.'

'No. This is good enough for me. We've a quick escape if we need it,' she said.

He rolled his eyes. Why would they need to escape? This was a Mooralup school event, not a war zone. The woman was paranoid. She sat there tense and expectant. He could feel the energy rolling off her in waves as they waited for the kids to come on stage.

As the curtains went up, he could feel

her tightly wired body relax a smidgeon and when Annie sang her solo pitch perfect, he felt a shift in her body. He glanced at her. A smile lit her face and there was a sparkle of a tear.

Her hands were clenched in her lap, but as the evening unfolded, she relaxed. Sam studied those small, pink hands. They begged to be held. Heck, he hadn't wanted to hold a woman's hand for a long time. The thought persisted and became a pressing need. Under the cover of darkness, he reached over and took her hand in his. She jumped at the unexpected gesture. His eyes sought hers. He half expected her to pull away, but instead her fingers curled around his. He smiled and she smiled too, shy and sweet.

'Proud, mama,' he whispered and brought her hand to his lips. He would have leaned into her and kissed her lips too, but this wasn't the time or the place. Maybe later, tonight, once they were at the cottage. The evening held warm promise.

'Al, what are you doing here?' Sam jumped down from the tractor after feeding the Murray Greys. It was a week after the play and Sam was feeling pretty content with life. The girls were happy and Ria was more relaxed. They were growing closer, sharing the occasional kiss when the girls weren't around. It was hell pacing the passion, but Sam had hopes that things would work out just peachy for them. Ria just needed a little time. 'Everything OK, mate? There're no fires?' And Sam automatically scanned the horizon for tell-tale signs of smoke.

'No. There's a prescribed burn the other side of town but that's contained.'

'Good. Then what?' And Sam felt a shift in his gut as he watched his friend's expression change. He knew he wasn't going to like the answer.

Al licked his lips. 'I'm sorry, mate. I was right.'

'About?' But he knew this was about Ria. Why else would Al be at the farm in uniform?

'The report came through this morning.'

'So what's she done?'

'Her name's Belle Bright.'

He tried not to let it get to him but, hell, why hadn't she told him she had a fake name? Why couldn't she have trusted him? He thought they were sharing something special. But, as galling as it seemed, he guessed not.

He gave Al a level look. 'So she changed her name. She probably had a good reason.'

'Well, yes, she did. The alleged murder of her husband and his business partner. We've arrested her on suspicion of said murders.'

'What?' That was a sucker punch to the guts.

'She's a husband killer, Sam. I thought you'd be better off hearing it from me, considering your relationship with her.'

'She's no killer, Al.' But was she? Good grief! And he had a flashback to the axe flying through the air with force, twice.

189

'You're not thinking with your head, mate. You've got the hots for her and can't think straight. Too much cake in my opinion.' And he gave a ghost of a smile. 'I'm sorry.'

'Has she admitted to it?'

'No. She swears she's innocent.'

'Then she is. If Ria said she didn't kill him, then, she didn't. Tell me what happened.'

'I'm not allowed to but I'll keep you posted on the general outcome. A Perth detective has been brought in to question her.'

'I'm convinced she hasn't done anything wrong. I know her husband was abusive, but murdering him? I don't think so.'

'I can't discuss it, Sam. But I'll do my best for her. Of course, if she's guilty, the law is the bottom line. I'm straight as a die. You know that.'

'Yeah. I know, mate. But be kind to her.'

'We don't go in for police brutality in Mooralup,' Al said dryly.

'What about the girls?'

'We have a family liaison officer with them at the station.'

'Can I see her? And the girls?'

'Maybe the kids. I'll see what I can do. Oh, and you may want to know the girls actual names. The oldest one is Hannah. The little one, Elspeth.'

After Al had left, Sam went to his computer. He typed in Belle Bright and added 'murder' and 'husband' and then hit the search button.

He sat back heavily as the screen filled with a picture of a dark haired Ria. Except that it wasn't. It was Belle Bright. So she'd worn her hair long and dark. It suited her better than the peroxide crop cut. She wasn't wearing glasses in the photo, but then Sam already knew they were fake. Well, the clues had been there all along, He'd just refused to acknowledge them.

There were two photos of the girls. They had the same dark hair as their mother. Bess — Elspeth — was missing her two front teeth. And there was a picture of Xander Bright, a handsome and debonair businessman, and a blurry photo of his associate Camelo Milo.

He read the article. Once he'd finished, he decided to keep his gun locked up. Just as a precaution. Maybe he'd lock up the axe too.

12

Belle sat in the small cell-like interview room at Busabarup Police Station. She clasped her hands tightly in front of her and stared tensely at Al, ignoring the tall dark detective sitting next to him who was giving her the evil eye.

Belle's neck and shoulders were tight, her stomach nauseous and her head pounded. She thought she was going to be sick and fought the prickling sensation. This couldn't be happening. She was a normal person, from a normal background. Murder was an alien concept in her world. Until twelve weeks ago, when her world was turned upside down and inside out and murder was slammed down bang in the middle.

'Your finger prints were on the gun that killed him,' said DI Steele in a cool hard voice. Belle stared at him in disbelief. 'That's impossible. I did not kill my husband.'

'They were there. Plain as plain, Mrs Bright.'

'But I didn't touch the gun. Camelo Milo, Xander's business partner was holding it.'

'Did you see him shoot your husband?'
'No.' 'I thought not. There were no other prints on the gun but yours. How do you explain that?'

She frowned and thought for a moment. 'I suppose,' she said slowly. 'I must have picked it up when I cleaned Xander's office.'

DI Steele wasn't impressed. 'Good try.' And he gave three slow hand claps.

She scowled at him, irritated by his attitude. 'Or they could have got there when we packed up our house to move to Sydney. I don't know. It wasn't as if I handled his gun on a regular basis.'

'And yet, if handling it was such a rare occurrence, you don't remember doing so?'

'No.'

'So tell me, why did he have a gun?'
To protect him from his low life cohorts!

Belle wanted to shout. Instead she said, 'I have no idea. I never thought to ask him. He'd always had one and so I accepted the status quo.'

'Can you shoot?'

'I didn't shoot Xander. He was already dying when I got there.'

'To hand him divorce papers.'

'Well, yes.'

'Why were you divorcing him?'

'It's private.'

'This is a murder investigation. Nothing is private anymore.'

'He was becoming irrational.'

Steele raised his eyebrows sceptically.

Belle sighed. 'And he was spending time with other women.'

'So you two weren't in a good place. You hated each other. You had motive.'

'I didn't hate him, DI Steele.'

'You wanted to divorce him,' he pointed out.

'I had fallen out of love with him, which I had done a long time ago, but I wasn't going to shoot him for failing to sign the divorce paperwork. There are less extreme ways to get a signature.'

'Such as?'

'Negotiation.' Though Xander had point blank refused to go to counselling. He'd reckoned their marriage was good enough. That they didn't need anyone meddling in their affairs. He'd promised to stop sleeping with other women. But he hadn't kept that promise. Or any of his other promises.

'Maybe he goaded you? Got you mad?'

'No. That's not what happened.'

He carried on, 'And because you knew about his gun, you took it from the desk and shot him.'

'He didn't keep it in the desk.'

'Ah.' DI Steele gave a supercilious smile. 'You knew where he kept it.'

'Of course I did. I helped set up the office. I worked there sometimes. And I cleaned it.'

'Even though you were estranged.'

'Neither of us had left the family home. We still shared the house.'

'And bedroom?'

'Is this relevant?'

'Just answer the question, Mrs Bright.'

'Yes.'

'Was he OK about the divorce?'

'No.'

'So he wouldn't sign the documents?'

'He didn't know I was coming in with the papers. He didn't have a chance to voice his opinion one way or the other about signing them. I told you before, he was already dying when I got there. I tried to save him, for heavens sake! I tried to ring for an ambulance.'

Belle vividly recalled the warm sticky blood. There'd been so much of it. She had a flashback of her feelings of inadequacy and helplessness to stem the flow. She quickly raised her hand to her mouth, forcing down the sudden rise of bile.

'That's what you'd have us believe. I think you're guilty, Mrs Bright. You shot your husband.'

'I did not kill my husband, DI Steele,' she mumbled through her fingers. 'I feel sick. I need the bathroom.'

The two men exchanged glances.

'This way,' Al said and escorted her to the restroom where a woman officer took over.

When Belle returned a few minutes later, DI Steele was pacing the room. He stopped moving and gazed at her coolly. 'Feeling better, Mrs Bright?'

'Not really.' She sat down shakily.

'Are you well enough to go on?' said Al, compassion in his eyes.

'Of course she is,' said Steele. 'It's an act.'

'Sir, with due respect, let Mrs Bright answer.'

Steele waved his hand impatiently.

'Yes, I'll carry on with the interview. Thank you for asking, but I want to get this over and done with. I need to get back to my daughters.'

'You'll be here a while yet,' said DI Steele.

Belle gave him a withering glare.

'Let's resume, shall we?' he said and read out the time and who was present for the tape and then said, 'Was your husband violent towards you, Mrs

198

Bright?'

She squeezed shut her eyes. 'Sometimes. Mainly verbally. Occasionally physically.'

'So were you defending yourself that day?'

She snapped her eyes open. 'No! I did not kill my husband!'

'You're lying.'

'I didn't kill him. It was Milo. He had the gun.'

Steele snorted in derision. 'You expect me to believe that? Then explain to me why Camelo Milo is dead?'

'Dead?' Belle was suddenly blindsided. 'How could he be?'

'He was found in his office.'

'What?' The earth tilted. There was a roaring in her head as Belle struggled to process the information. There had been someone else lurking in the office that afternoon? A cold chill blew through her, turning her blood to ice. She could have been murdered that day too! The girls could have lost both parents in one fell swoop!

No! Don't go there, Belle!

'So,' said Steele. 'Would you like to reconsider your answer, Mrs Bright?'

'I didn't kill him.' She clutched the edge of the table, her knuckles bone white with the pressure.

'Why did you shoot Milo?'

'I don't believe this! I didn't shoot anyone! I'm not a murderer!'

She had a horrified thought . . . If Milo was dead, who was sending her the threatening text messages? Who else was out to get her? This couldn't be happening.

'But you ran away from the crime scene and have been on the run ever since, taking on a new identity for you and the kids, living a lie. In my book that smacks of guilt.'

'I ran because Milo threatened to kill us.'

'Right.' The word came out flat, showing the DI's lack of belief in her story.

'He's a dangerous man. He embroiled my husband in his shady business deals. He wasn't a man to cross. I was scared of him.'

'Right. So how come he let you get away, if he was the one holding the gun and threatening you? Hmm?'

'I hit him.'

Steele snorted. 'With no disrespect, you don't look like someone who could deck a man. Which brings us back to you shooting him.'

'I hit him with a rock.'

Now Steele laughed out loud and slapped the table with his open palm. 'There just happened to be a convenient rock lying around in an office. Pull the other one, Mrs Bright!'

'My husband had a rock paperweight on his desk. My oldest daughter had painted it for him for Father's Day. I used that,' she said coldly.

'And did what with it?'

She frowned, trying to remember. 'I dropped it and ran.'

'And you reckon Milo was still alive when you left?' chipped in Al.

'Yes. I hit him once and stunned him, but there was no way I hit him hard enough to kill him. Are you really sure he's dead?' Belle rubbed her temples, reliving that awful day. 'Because he's been sending me threatening messages. Where did you find him?'

'We're the one asking the questions,' said the detective sullenly.

'It's OK,' said Al, again interrupting his senior officer. 'Here, Ria . . . sorry, Belle.' And he shoved a sheaf of graphic crime scene photos across the desk towards her.

Belle stared unflinchingly at Xander's body. She had compassion for the man who'd once been her husband. But she also felt regret that things hadn't worked out and anger that he'd hurt her so badly over the years and now, in death, he was still hurting her and the children. She found it incredibly hard to forgive him for putting their girls and their unborn baby in so much danger.

Without thinking, she put her hand protectively over her belly as she shuffled through the photos on the desk with her other hand. She stopped when she came to the pictures of the second body. It was lying by Milo's desk, staring at the ceiling, except there were no eyes. The man's face was a bloodied mess. There was no way of making out who it was. She looked at the photos carefully and frowned. She raised her head and met Al's inquiring gaze. 'This isn't Milo.' She held out the print to Al.

'The hell it isn't,' said the detective. 'You expect us to take your word for it?'

'It's not Cam Milo.'

'How can you tell? He hasn't a face. You shot it off, remember?'

Belle ignored his last comment. 'Milo was wearing a black suit. This guy's in light grey. I doubt if Milo would have changed suits, even if there would have been time before the emergency services arrived. Why do you think it was Milo?'

'From the ID in his wallet.'

'Which you took at face value?' Belle said with a twisted smile. 'You bother to check?'

'There seemed no reason to. It was his

private office. It was logical that it was him, what with his partner lying dead in his own office too.'

'I suggest that was the wrong assumption to make. Milo could have easily planted his ID on the other guy and then disappeared. I would also suggest you find that paperweight and see if there's a DNA match with the dead man or not.'

'Don't get clever with me, Mrs Bright.'

Al cleared his throat and intervened. 'Who is this man then?'

Belle glanced at the bloodied corpse again. She pushed the photo away with the tip of her finger. 'I have no idea, Al.'

'You'd better tell me about these messages,' Al said, almost ignoring his senior officer.

* * *

After 24 hours, Belle was released on bail. Shell-shocked from the experience, she felt wrung out and exhausted. Her bail conditions included surrendering hers and the girls' passports, staying at the cottage, and reporting to the Mooralup Police Station every day. Now, all she wanted to do was go home and hide away from the world with her girls.

Would she be able to? Would she be safe? Belle was scared that, now the police had found her, Milo would too. DI Steele might be unconvinced the body wasn't Milo's, but Belle knew otherwise. It didn't help her peace of mind that Al had indicated that if the body wasn't Milo, then the police had no idea of his whereabouts. They apparently knew little about him, only scant facts gleaned from the caretaker of the office block. With no next-of-kin known, the police hadn't bothered to dig too deeply into his life. They'd presumed it was a cut and dried case, with Milo getting in the crossfire of a domestic, and Belle as prime suspect.

Belle stepped out of the Busabarup Police Station and into the powerful midday heat. The glare momentarily blinded her. She lifted her face to the sun, enjoying its warm kiss on her chilled skin. She savoured it for several seconds then lowered her head to look for Sam. Al had told her he'd be waiting outside, just after he'd told her, in no uncertain terms, that Sam had gone surety for her bail bond and that she'd better not betray his faith in her, or else she had Al to answer to. It was touching to witness the fierce loyalty of friends, and she was humbled that she was included in Sam's friendship. She'd presumed he would have distanced himself from the accused husband killer, but instead he was supporting her.

She spotted Sam almost immediately; tall and straight and striking. He was standing on the opposite side of the road, staring right at her.

As her eyes rested on him, he lifted his hand in the barest of acknowledgements. Even from this distance she could tell he was wary, his expression buttoned down. Was he regretting getting involved? She didn't blame him. She was bad news. In her defence, she had warned him.

Sam glanced left and right and then strode confidently across the road towards her. He stopped a few feet away. The space between them yawned a chasm. Their eyes met and she felt her heart beat in her mouth. He was so gorgeous and solid and reliable and she didn't deserve him to be here. She was so very grateful and thankful that he was.

'I told you you'd regret knowing me,' she said in a small voice, breaking the tense silence.

He didn't say anything, simply opened his arms. She hesitated.

'Come here, you stupid girl. How could I ever regret knowing you?' he said, his voice throbbing with suppressed emotion.

'Oh Sam. I'm so glad you're here.' She gave an involuntary sob as she stepped into his embrace.

He cuddled her to him, kissing the top of her head. 'Can't think where else I'd rather be.'

'And thank you for going bail for me,' she said, the words muffled in his shirt.

'My pleasure, honey. Any time. Now come on. Let's get you home.'

'It's all such a mess.'

'Don't worry. We'll survive this.'

'Maybe.' Belle doubted it. Cam Milo was out there somewhere, wanting his money. They could all get hurt. She shouldn't have embroiled Sam. But it was too late now.

'Where are the girls? Are they OK?'

'They're fine and already at home.'

'On their own?' She said with an edge of panic.

'No, of course not. Relax. They were being cared for by a family liaison officer but my sister has come to stay for a while. She's with them. It's all fine, Ria.' Though Belle saw a tightening of his jaw. He wasn't happy. Because of her false name? Because of the kids?

'Actually, my name's Belle. Belle Bright,' she said in a rush.

'So I gathered from Al.' And from the article, which had also filled him in on her background so that he now knew so much more about this complex woman.

'I'm sorry I didn't tell you. But I never expected this — us — to happen. I'd never done the fugitive thing before.'

'You should have trusted me.'

'Put yourself in my shoes, Sam. My daughters' lives were on the line.' Belle's voice caught. 'I think you would have done the same.'

'I would have told you.'

'I did what I thought best for my girls' sakes.'

His jaw flexed. 'And yours.'

Belle stared levelly at him. 'Yes and mine too. Survival kicked in. I would do it all over again.'

The breath whooshed out between his teeth. 'This is crazy. Look, it doesn't matter. You did it. And now I know who you really are.'

Belle Bright of Sussex, aged thirty, married at eighteen, who emigrated three months ago and is now wanted by the police for murdering her husband and his business partner .

'Did Al tell you why I was arrested?'

Sam swept a look about him and then fleetingly down at Belle. 'Yes, but this is not the place to discuss it. Tell me in the truck.'

He took her by the arm and led her to his parked ute. Old Derek was sitting in the back with his pink tongue lolling out of his mouth, dribbling. His head bobbed back and forth as he watched the action, obviously enjoying the unexpected day out. He wagged his tail when he saw his master.

Sam opened the door for Belle to get in. 'What should I call you? Do you prefer Belle or Ria?'

'Belle. Though please call me Ria in public. I still don't want people to know my true identity.'

'Belle it is, then. It's a pretty name. I like it.'

Sam navigated out of town and headed home.

'Now tell me everything. Al only gave me the basics otherwise he was all silent professionalism. I need to know who you are and what's going on if we're going to survive this.'

Quietly and hesitantly, Belle told Sam about her rocky marriage, the family's new start in Australia, the bad business partnership that ended in Xander's murder and their panicked flight to get away from Cam Milo.

'The police think I killed Xander because he wouldn't give me a divorce. As if I could murder the father of my children? It's insane!'

Sam took his hand off the steering wheel to give hers a squeeze. 'They'll find the right person. Have faith. Al's on the job. He's a good bloke. One of the best.'

'He might be, but he's not heading the investigation. This DI Steele is and he lives up to his name; cold, sharp and deadly. He thinks I'm guilty of murdering Xander and this other bloke who was found dead in Milo's office. I don't feel confident I'll be exonerated.'

'Of course you will. The evidence will back you.'

'I hope so but in the meantime Cam Milo is out there somewhere. The police have no idea where because they thought the second body was him and hadn't investigated further. I'm scared, Sam. Milo's a dangerous man. He has contacts in the criminal world. When I first met you I thought you were a hit-man hired by him.'

'Really? Good grief, no wonder you looked terrified! But, honey, you should be safe in Mooralup. We're not exactly the hub of crime.'

'Don't bank on it.'

'I have my gun and you're a dab-hand with an axe. We'll be fine, Belle.'

Although he had made it sound like a joke, Belle felt he'd meant it. But as far as she was concerned, it didn't bode well.

13

As they drove towards Mooralup, Belle grew silent. Sam left her to her own thoughts and focussed on what would happen next.

Should he get Ria — Belle — and the girls to move into his place? No. Bad idea. He didn't think they were quite at that stage in their relationship. They might never be, if she was found guilty . . .

No. He couldn't believe it. But if Belle had done it, there would have been great provocation. The look Belle sometimes had in her eyes he'd seen many times before; his mother had worn the same look on countless occasions . . . fear, shame, desperation. Thinking of his mother dredged up memories he usually left buried deep in the darkness, but sometimes they exploded to the surface.

His early childhood hadn't been that rosy with a disciplinarian father, and then after his dad had died, his mother had remarried, far too quickly in Sam's opinion. His stepfather had a temper that could sear steak and Sam had copped vicious beatings during his teen years. And it wasn't just him that had been beaten. The rest of the family had lived in constant fear.

Sam was chucked out at sixteen and had joined the army. As soon as he'd done his sign-up time, he'd come back for the reckoning. That was the day he broke his stepfather's jaw and sent him packing to save his mum and three sisters from any further violence.

Now one of those sisters, Merrily, the oldest, was ensconced at home, which was tricky. He loved her dearly, but Sam couldn't help but wonder why she had decided now, of all times, to come and stay? Because, Sam guessed, she'd heard via the jungle drums that things were going down in Mooralup and she should get herself there to protect her big brother from the fallout. She was a warrior when it came to her family, just as he was. He really couldn't blame her, but it could well end in tears.

Merrily had breezed in the day before, with two heavy suitcases and her soppy black Labrador.

'So what game are you playing, bro?' she'd said on arrival.

'Nice to see you too, Merry. Long time no see. How are things?' He'd kissed her cheek and let the dog jump up for a slob-bery welcome.

Merrily had ignored his sarcasm and waded straight into what was bothering her.

'A woman with two kids and a murder charge hanging around her neck? Have you rocks in your head, Sam Taggart? Or somewhere else, hmm?' She'd glanced at her dog. 'Down, Dotty!'

The dog slobbered some more and then sat with a big grin on her black face, her brown eyes flitting from one to the other of them, her thick black tail thump-thumping on the floorboards.

'The woman needs support. She's also my neighbour. It's a done deal,' he'd said mildly.

'I've heard she's baking you cakes, bro. Can you deny that?'

'The cake isn't a metaphor, sis. So far she's made made me jam sponge, banana bread and a fruit loaf. In fact I have some fruit loaf left it you would like to try a slice with a cuppa?'

'Stop trying to change the subject. You're a commitment phobe, Sam. So what's the deal?'

'I wouldn't describe myself that way.'

'You should. You've never had a girl-friend longer than it takes to . . . ' she'd paused dramatically. 'To bake a cake.'

'You're forgetting the delectable Char-lotte.'

'Hah. You were relieved — no down-right happy — when she ran off. The only duff note was her taking your dog and best mate with her. So why is this Ria Carlson so different? How come you're suddenly discovering you've a romantic heart beating in your manly chest? Is she pretty?'

'I think so. She's as sweet as . . . as a sun-ripened peach.'

'Oh dear!' She'd given a deep belly laugh. 'I can't wait to see this gorgeous girl who's captured your staid bachelor heart. But I hear she's in custody . . . that's a bummer!'

'And her daughters are with a police officer at the Swifts' shearers' cottage.'

'That dump? How old are they?'

'Oh didn't you get that bit of information? You're losing your touch, Merry.'

'Sam,' she'd said warningly.

'They're seven and ten.'

'Poor kids. They'll be missing their ma. Let's spring 'em and bring them back here.'

And that was why Sam loved his sister. She was spontaneous, big-hearted and willing to put her thoughts into action. She was also an advocate for the underdog. But he was unsure if she had Ria — Belle — down as a victim or perpetrator. She might be out to save only him — and possibly Belle's girls. He'd have to watch her.

Now, as he turned into the farm driveway, Belle said, 'Aren't we going to the cottage?'

'The girls stayed here last night. Merrily thought it a good idea as we have TV to distract them. The liaison officer was finding it hard keeping them amused as you didn't have one.'

'That's fair enough. They can get demanding.'

The girls spilled out of the house, along with Dotty the dog, and clung to Belle, talking fast and furiously about how marvellous it was at the farm. They'd been making pikelets with Merrily and flown home-made newspaper kites until one got stuck up a tree and the other got eaten by the dog. While they gabbled on, pulling Belle towards the kitchen, Merrily, stood quietly on the verandah. She sought out Sam and gave him a slightly raised eyebrow. It was crunch time.

'Hey, Belle, before you go in with the kids, I'd like you to meet my sister, Merrily.'

Belle visibly straightened her shoulders and then turned towards Merrily, extricating herself from her daughters.

'Thank you for looking after my girls,' said Belle politely. She held out her hand and shook Merrily's. 'I do so appreciate it. It hasn't been an easy time for them.'

'No drama.' Merrily gave a breezy smile. 'I was passing by and thought I could help.'

It was Sam's turn to raise a brow. His sister had driven a solid four hours to get to his door and had brought enough clothes to last a month. No way had it been a spontaneous gesture. It'd been a meticulously planned coup!

The girls reclaimed Belle's attention. 'We had a police woman looking after us,' said Hannah.

'That was nice,' said Belle.

'It wasn't,' said Elspeth. 'She was scary. It's better here. Sam taught us how to play poker.'

'Did he now?' So when had Mr Taggart become Sam, and why poker? 'Was that strictly necessary? Poker's not exactly a child's game.'

'In my defence, it's the only card game I know.'

'We shall have to teach you Donkey then,' said Belle. 'But on another day. Let's gather everything up and go home.'

'You don't want to stay?' said Sam. It popped out before he'd really thought it through. When had he changed his mind? But he had. He didn't want her to go.

Her expression became evasive. 'We need to get back to normality.'

'OK Your call. But it's all set up here for the girls and it won't take long to make you up a bed too.' He was disappointed she didn't want to stay under his protection.

'I think it's for the best.'

'Can we eat the pikelets?' said Hannah.

'Of course we can,' said Merrily. 'I'll pop the kettle on and you girls get out plates and butter.'

'And strawberry jam,' said Elspeth.

Belle felt out manoeuvred but, as graciously as she could, she sat at the kitchen table and waited for afternoon tea. She made the right noises as she ate the pikelets for the girls' sakes but the food could have been cardboard for all she cared. She needed to get home and make plans.

Sam leaned towards her and whispered in her ear, 'You'd be more comfortable here. Why don't you reconsider?'

She turned and gave him a clear, level look. 'And break my bail terms the very first night I'm released? I don't think so. I'd go to jail and you'd lose the bond money. But thanks all the same, Sam. I appreciate the offer.'

Later, the children gathered up their belongings and Sam drove the Bright family to the cottage. The girls raced off to check on the chickens.

Sam turned to Belle. 'You won't do anything stupid, will you?' he said, hating having to ask, but feeling her withdrawal. 'Like running away.'

'Are you worried about your money, Sam?' She said dryly.

'The money's neither here nor there. But I mean it, Belle, don't go disappearing on me.'

'I won't go unless I'm forced to and then I'll do whatever I think best under the circumstances. That's the best I can offer. If I do have to run, I'll pay you back the money somehow.'

'The money doesn't matter. You do. I'm here for you, Belle. Please, don't run out on me.'

She fleetingly raised her eyes to his. 'Thank you, Sam. I wish I'd met you a lifetime ago. Things could have been so different.'

'It's not too late.' Sam took her hand and held it firmly against his cheek, then brought it to his lips and kissed her palm. 'We could have the rest of our lives together, honey. Just say the word.'

Belle blinked in surprise. 'You mean that? Even with all this trouble you still care?'

'Absolutely.'

Before Belle could respond, a piercing scream rent the air.

'What the hell?' said Sam, spinning around.

'Oh my god, it's Milo!' said Belle and

they legged it to the chicken run, meeting the girls running helter-skelter towards them. They crashed into Belle and clung to her like limpets, squealing at the top of their lungs.

'What's up?' demanded Sam, preparing to do battle and wondering if he could cope.

'There's a dinosaur in the chickens!' said Elspeth.'I put my hand under Petula to check for eggs and touched it. It was horrible!' And she burrowed into Belle's embrace. 'It scared me.'

'Petula?' Sam queried.

'One of the hens,' explained Belle.

'Of course she is.' Sam could feel his heart rate beginning to return to normal. All this talk of murder and hit-men was making him as paranoid as Belle! Not a good feeling. 'This dinosaur? Would it be a bobtail, by any chance?'

'What's that?' said Hannah.

'A big fat lizard with a blue tongue and a blunt tail? About this big?' and he held out his hands.

'I guess.' She looked doubtful. 'But it

was quite dark in there and so I didn't get a really good look. We just ran.'

'I'll go and check him out.'

'Be careful, Sam,' said Belle, her voice still wobbly from the adrenalin rush. 'It might bite.'

'It's fine. He's not dangerous.' He gave her a reassuring smile, inwardly relieved that it wasn't anything more sinister than a reptile. 'But I will move him otherwise he'll eat all your eggs.'

The girls huddled close to their mum, and Sam left without a chance to talk to Belle again.

* * *

'So,' Merrily confronted Sam the moment he got back to the farm. 'Is it yours?'

Sam blinked. 'You know about the baby?' He sounded incredulous.

'I'm a woman, dummy. Is that why you're so keen to help this woman?'

'No. We don't have sort of relationship.' Yet.

'I hope you know what you're doing.'

'I don't, as a matter of fact but I'm doing it anyway. So how long do you intend on staying?'

'For as long as it takes, big bro, and not before. You need my protection.'

'Like hell I do.'

'You're a big softie and that woman knows it.'

'She needs me, Merry.'

'Oh, boy! Looks like I'm going to be here quite a while then.'

Sam rolled his eyes and pushed past her into the house. That's all he needed in the mix, a sister bodyguard . . . and her crazy dog.

* * *

Rhys Steele parked outside the cottage. He killed the engine and listened. A kookaburra was laughing its head off as it balanced on top of the chimney. A second kookaburra joined in and they proceeded to have an hysterical bout of cackling.

Good for them. But Steele didn't feel as jolly as the laughing birds. He was nursing a hangover after spending the night carousing with the Mooralup cop. That Al Tonkin certainly knew how to have a good time! Apparently it wasn't often that the older bloke was away from his family and he'd decided to make the most of it, at Steele's expense. Jeepers, he was corked!

Steele left the car parked in the oak tree's shade and looked about, feeling as inspired as a wet sock. The place was pretty darn derelict. In his opinion, it needed to be razed to the ground. Once upon a time someone had tried to grow a garden. There were skeletal remnants of flower beds with an odd leggy rose still blooming against the odds. At least the glory vine and plumbago were flourishing, but then, it was hard to kill them. It reminded him of his grandma's place. He hadn't thought about the old girl for years.

Steele knocked on the door. There was no reply. He marched around to the back and found Belle hanging out washing. 'Mrs Bright.'

She gave him a wary glance. 'DI Steele. I wasn't expecting to see you.'

'I've a few questions.' He opened a notebook. 'How did you leave your house in Sydney?'

'In a hurry.'

'So you emptied drawers and cupboards?'

'No.' She gave him a puzzled look. 'I grabbed our passports, paperwork and a few essentials. I wasn't going to hang about with Milo on my heels. As I said at the interview, I took his threats seriously. Even if you don't.'

'So it was tidy when you left it?'

'It was as tidy as any other suburban family home on a busy weekday. Are you telling me you found it otherwise?'

'Unless you're a very messy family, I would say it had been ransacked. There was paperwork and stuff strewn about the rooms.'

Belle massaged her temples. 'But why?'

'You tell me?'

She sighed and dropped her hands. 'I suppose Camelo Milo was looking for something?' His money? His key? 'No one else would be interested in us. Hardly anybody knows us. The only other explanation would be a burglar. I really don't know.'

Steele made some notes. 'Has Milo contacted you since we talked to you?'

She turned and walked past him into the house. She took her phone from a drawer, hit some buttons and then handed it to him . . .

Where are you, tramp? I will find you.

'That's why I would appreciate you not giving out my real name. I don't want him finding me.'

'He hasn't been seen since your husband's death. It's almost as if he doesn't exist.' He waited a beat. 'Or is dead. Face it, Mrs Bright. Anyone could have sent those messages.' He gave her back the phone.

Belle rolled her eyes in exasperation. 'I didn't shoot him! Look, DI Steele, if a new immigrant with no contacts or family network and two young children, can hide as long as I have, then it'll be even easier for him as a single man with underworld contacts.'

'We'll carry on investigating.' Though he wasn't thrilled about that. In his book, it was a waste of time. The woman was guilty. Case closed.

'Good. Because I'm scared, DI Steele. I'm scared for my girls.'

'Perhaps you should stay with friends. Or family,' he said dismissively. He didn't believe there was a problem. He reckoned it was Milo on the morgue slab and that she just had some two-bit stalker winding her up.

'You've taken my passport.'

'I meant in this country.'

'Then I stay here at the cottage, which is part of my bail conditions anyway. I don't have a network of family and friends in Australia. I've nowhere else to go.' And she resolutely blocked the idea that she could find sanctuary with Sam Taggart. The poor bloke didn't deserve to be burdened.

'I'll take your phone and look into these messages,' said Steele. 'Find out whose sending them. To put your mind at rest.'

'You do that.' She slapped the phone into his hand. 'But all you'll find is Milo.'

'Maybe. I'll be in touch.'

'I can't wait.'

* * *

Belle hunkered down among the tomato plants, the foliage making her skin itch. She fossicked through the leaves, picking the last of the season's Romas, filling the box with the firm pear-shaped fruit. The sun was hotter than she'd expected, considering it was almost autumn. Her shirt stuck to her back with sweat. She should have worn a hat. She should have brought along her water bottle. Actually, she shouldn't be here.

Staying home hadn't been an option, however, even though she felt emotionally exhausted from the police interrogation and physically tired from catching up with the hand-washing and housework. She could have taken advantage of Sam's washing machine except she didn't want to encroach, especially with his sister in the house. Merrily was a force of nature. She didn't know if the woman really liked her, which was understandable given the situation.

Belle picked steadily and then rose to her feet to move to the next row. There was a sudden stab of pain in her abdomen. She gasped and doubled over, clutching her belly, and dropped the box of tomatoes, the fruit bouncing in all directions.

She sat down hard, feeling faint and nauseous. She could feel wet heat between her legs. Blood began to soak through the fabric of her jeans and she gave an involuntary sob. The baby!

'Are you OK?' Sam called out. He was carrying two mugs of coffee. He took one look at Belle and tossed them down, running to her side. 'Let's get you straight to hospital! Don't argue, Belle!'

'The girls?'

'Don't worry. There's Merrily.' He bent down. 'Put your arms around my neck.'

'You can't carry me,' she said, her voice sounding tinny and a long way off.

'Watch me, baby. Now, here we go . . . h'up!'

'The tomatoes . . . '

'To hell with the tomatoes.'

He carried her through the vegetable garden, stomping over the vines and crunching tomatoes underfoot, and took her to the ute. He clicked the seatbelt around her. 'Steady as we go,' he said. 'Don't worry, honey. It'll all be fine. '

She squeezed shut her eyes. 'I hope so.' And she held her hands over her belly, praying hard.

★ ★ ★

'There's a chance we've saved the baby,' said the duty doctor later that night. 'But it's still touch and go. I want you to stay in hospital for the next few days and we'll see what happens. Now, whose your GP?'

'I don't have one. I'm new to town. I haven't got around to it yet. I've had other things on my mind.' Her hands were clenched at her sides and she felt resentful and worried and terrified that she would lose her precious baby.

'More important than your baby? I'd advise you to get on to it, Mrs Carlson. You don't want to take any more risks.'

She shot him a mutinous look as he left to see another patient. 'That man has no idea what I've been going through,' she said through clenched teeth. 'I didn't purposely put my baby at risk.'

The nurse who was fussing about the room put a comforting hand on Belle's shoulder. 'We're not the enemy, Ria.'

Belle leaned back into the snowy white pillows. 'I know. I'm sorry.'

'We're all here to help you. Including your gorgeous neighbour whose been waiting patiently to see you.'

'Sam's still here?'

'Oh yes, darlin'. Striding up and down

that waiting room, making deep tracks in the floor tiles. He's a lovely man. You've stolen a march on the rest of us Mooralup women!'

'It wasn't intentional,' she gave a wan smile. 'He's sort of adopted my family.'

'He's a good bloke. I went to school with him.'

'You did?'

'Oh yes, and I'll let you in on a secret, Ria, he was the dorkiest kid in school. His clothes were too big so he looked like a scarecrow — got teased for it too. Then he had a growth spurt and the clothes were all too small for him so he still looked like a scarecrow.'

'He doesn't seem too fussed about his appearance even now.'

'True. He was a quiet lad,' said the nurse. 'But a real scrapper. If anyone upset him or his sisters, he was ready with his fists, even if it meant he got hurt or got in trouble with the teachers.'

'A bit of a hero, then.'

'Too right. Shall I send him in?'

Belle nibbled her bottom lip. 'How do

I look?'

'Washed out. Or pale and interesting, as my old mum used to say.' She grinned. 'But I don't think it really matters what you look like. He's looking pretty terrible himself. I'll tell him he can have five minutes, and then you must rest, luvvie.'

Sam hovered at the entrance to the small four-bed ward. The other three beds were temporarily empty.

'How are you feeling, honey?' he said.

'Tired. Teary. Hopeful my baby's OK.'

'You gave us all a scare.'

He came in and drew up a chair next to the bed. He took her hand and kissed her knuckles and then held it against his chin which was golden and scratchy and in need of a shave.

Belle gave a faint smile and squeezed his hand. 'I gave myself one.'

'They said you'll need total bed rest for a few days once you leave here, so you'd best move to my place.' He held up his other hand to silence her immediate protest. 'I've an indoor toilet. I don't want you staggering along that broken concrete path to your outside dunny. So no arguments, Belle.'

'But what about my bail conditions?'

'I'll have a chat with Al and see if he can swing it for you.'

'You're always looking after us.' And the tears sparkled on her dark lashes.

'Yep, it seems to be getting that way,' and he smiled. 'I don't mind a bit. Now get some sleep and don't worry about the girls. Merrily has come into her own. And so has Dotty.'

14

DI Steele stood in the middle of the courtyard of Sam Taggart's farm house. A hairy ball of legs, tail and ears bounced out to greet him. The black Labrador leapt at him, hitting him in the solar plexus with her front paws, and spraying his jacket with saliva as she barked excitedly.

'Down!' roared Steele, and the dog dropped. 'Sit!' he commanded and Dotty did. She sat, tongue lolling and her tail frantically wagging. 'Stay!' Dotty's backside waggled along with the tail, scuffing the dust.

'May I help you?' said a woman from the verandah. Her stance was combative with her hands on her hips and her face stern. She didn't sound as though she wanted to help anyone, least of all him.

'DI Steele,' he said. 'I believe Mrs Bright is staying here?'

'And?'

'And I would like to speak with her, if I may,' he said mildly.

'She's not up to it.'

'This is a murder investigation.' His voice sharpened. 'I need to speak to her.'

The woman looked mutinous. 'I'll ask her.'

Steele propelled himself forward and bounded up the verandah steps, almost tripping over the black Lab that had followed him. Obvious Dotty thought that if he could move, then so could she. 'How about I come too, Ms . . . ?'

She swung around to face him and held up her hand, which smacked him in the chest. 'How about you don't, DI Steele? Stay here.'

She didn't quite use the same tone of command Steele had used on the dog, but it wasn't far off, he realised, and was annoyed at the woman's temerity.

Satisfied the police detective was going to obey her, Merrily dropped her hand and disappeared into the house without introducing herself.

Steele glowered but stayed where he

was. He'd give her two minutes and then he'd go in after her.

Within moments she reappeared. 'OK. You can have five minutes. Max.'

He'd driven all the way from Busabarup. He intended to get more than five sodding minutes of Belle Bright's precious time!

'And your name is?' He inquired as he followed her into the house.

'Merrily Taggart.' She offered no other explanation.

'Any relation to Sam?'

She gave him a cool look. 'Sister.' And then she stepped back to let him into the room.

Belle was settled on a couch with her feet up. She was porcelain-pale and big-eyed. She looked more fragile than she had at the police station a week ago. She was either very sick or a good actress. Considering she'd managed to dodge the law for three months, he was leaning more to the latter.

'I'm sorry to intrude,' said Steele with a curt nod of his head.

'No, you're not,' said Merrily.

She had perched on the armrest of the couch. In her black leggings and blue sleeveless T-shirt, her golden hair secured in a messy knot on the top of her head, she looked like a manic fitness instructor with a demeanour of a sergeant major.

He flicked her an irritated glance and then focussed on Belle. He took his notebook from his case. Opening it, he said, 'This won't take long, Mrs Bright.'

'Good,' said Merrily.

Steele ignored her. 'I need you to tell me everything you know, however random, about Camelo Milo.'

'Why?' said Belle.

'I'm afraid we're still finding it hard to find anything on him.'

'That's because he's a slimy crook and, like Teflon, nothing sticks.'

'That's not helpful.'

'But true.'

'Mrs Bright, please. We really are trying to build a comprehensive profile on him but we've scant facts.'

'He's careful not to be in the limelight

or to incriminate himself, that's why.' She picked up and cushion and held it against her torso in a defensive, childish gesture and gave him a hostile glare. 'He uses greedy, dumb foot soldiers like my late husband to do his dirty work.'

'How did your husband and Milo meet?

'They met at a conference in the UK last September. Milo offered Xander a business partnership based in Sydney. Xander was keen to emigrate. It was all very fast. Milo organised our visas, tickets and accommodation. We arrived in Sydney on New Year's Eve.' She gave an involuntary shudder.

Steele made notes. 'So Milo is an Australian citizen, then?'

'He sponsored us so I believe he was. I never thought to ask. I wasn't that interested in him. Anyway, surely you can find more information about him through the DNA on the paperweight?'

'We only have your word that the paperweight actually exists.'

Belle raised her brows. 'Excuse me?'

'There was no paperweight found at the scene. I've double checked.'

'But it was a great big lump of Brighton rock painted with yellow and white daisies — and with blood on it! You couldn't miss it.'

'There was no rock, with blood on it or daisies or anything else.'

'I dropped it on the floor. Maybe it rolled under the desk?'

'There was no rock.'

'So why are you even bothering to look for Milo if you reckon I'm lying?' She huffed angrily. 'You've obviously decided that I murdered both him and Xander!'

'Because the other body wasn't Camelo Milo.'

That got Belle's attention. 'Ah. So now you know I was telling the truth! So who was it?'

Steele didn't look happy. 'A Nathaniel Thomas. Do you know him?'

'No.' Or did she? She racked her brains but couldn't quite pinpoint the name.

'He was reported missing by his family a couple of days ago, after he failed to turn up to a family wedding.'

'Why was he at the office?'

'He was a temporary employee from a recruitment agency.'

So he wasn't anyone she would have known from Milo's world. That was a relief. 'A temp doing what?'

'Reception and admin.'

'Really? That wasn't their usual practise.'

'Meaning?'

'Xander and Milo only employed blonde tottie. It suited their playboy image.' She gave a crooked smile. 'And it made working more fun, to quote my darling husband.' She couldn't keep the bitterness out of her voice. 'But I guess there wasn't a blonde available that day and they had to make do.' She suddenly looked down at her own hands, surprised by her own angry outburst. Quietly, she added, 'Poor Mr Thomas. He was in the wrong place at the wrong time.'

'You sure you didn't see him that day?'

'No. There was no one on reception and so I just went straight through, half thinking I would surprise Xander canoodling with the pretty receptionist of the day. Instead, there he was, bleeding out on the floor. And then Milo came out of his office with the gun. There was no sign of anyone else.'

'Hmm.' Steele was non-committal. 'Do you know the name of any of Milo's businesses apart from your husband's finance company?'

'Now you're asking . . . ' Belle thought hard for a minute or two and then listed as many as she could off the top of her head. They included various wine bars and tattoo and massage parlours throughout the city.

'Did you socialise with him?'

'Not if I could help it.'

'But you did?'

'Yes.' And she dropped her eyes and plucked at the dark green cushion.

'Mrs Bright?'

'He had an account at The Singing Chimp Hotel where he would wine and dine clients. I was asked — no, make that ordered — to go along sometimes

244

and be nice to them. It wasn't all it was cracked up to be. Sordid and nasty.'

Her eyes welled up despite her defiant air.

'That's enough!' said Merrily. 'You've over stayed your welcome, Steele.'

'So he pimped you out?' Steele said, ignoring Merrily again.

'Enough!' roared Merrily.

Steele held up his hand to silence her and Merry sprang to her feet, quivering outrage, looking as if she was going to deck him.

'Just one more minute,' he said, keeping one wary eye on Merry. 'Mrs Bright?'

'Not quite,' said Belle, holding her knuckles against her mouth. 'But it was degrading anyway. I was more of a hostess. I had to encourage them to drink. To have a good time. There were other girls who provided the 'extra' services. But not me. Though Milo made no secret of the fact he expected me to step up in time and become one of the escorts. But I drew the line at that.'

'Did your husband know how Milo

used you?'

'What do you think?' She snapped, her eyes glistening with her unshed tears, still appalled that her husband had condoned it.

'That's it, Steele. You're out of here!' Merrily moved between Belle and the detective.

'I'm just doing my job, Ms Taggart.'

'You've done it, buster. Now go!'

They squared off. Hot blue eyes challenging his cool silver.

'Look, lady, back off. This is a murder investigation. I'm fully entitled to be here.'

'I don't care. Belle is sick. The doc said she shouldn't be stressed and what are you doing, mate? You're stressing the hell outta her. Get out now, before I throw you out.'

'I could arrest you for obstructing a police officer, you know.'

'Just you try it.' And those hands went on to her hips with the loud message *don't mess with me, chum!*

Those blue eyes sparked and Steele

had the sudden crazy urge to laugh. She must have seen the twitch of his lips and flare of amusement in his eyes because her own eyes narrowed dangerously. With immense willpower, he managed to control his face and held up both hands in surrender.

'OK, lady. I'll take my leave. But I'll come back tomorrow when Mrs Bright will — I hope — be feeling a little better.'

'You do that.'

And hopefully you'll be feeling better too, he felt like saying. But instead, he said, 'Thank you for your time, Mrs Bright. Good day, Ms Taggart.'

Before he could leave, Sam came striding into the room with a purposeful, unfriendly air.

Great. Another angry Taggart. Just what I need! Steele thought.

'What's going on?' said Sam and he went immediately to kneel down beside Belle.

'DI Steele has been bullying Belle,' said Merrily with a ferocious stare.

'Oh, come on! That's a bit strong. I've

just talked to Mrs Bright, Mr Taggart, and now I'm leaving,' said Steele and exited before anyone else gave him any gyp.

Dotty followed him outside with her tail wagging.

Well, at least the dog liked him!

Sam slung his arm around Belle and turned to Merrily. 'What did he want?'

'To interview Belle.'

'But what did he want to know that upset you so much?' he asked Belle.

'Things about Milo,' she replied warily.

'OK.' He seemed a little perplexed. 'Well, don't get too het up, hon. The guy's just doing his job. You want him to find this Milo, which means he has to get as much information as possible and you're probably his best line of inquiry.'

Belle sent an imploring look at Merrily.

'Yes, but it's his attitude,' said Merrily smoothly. 'It's irritating.'

'Chill out, Merry. He's got to get answers. Cut the guy some slack.'

'He's a prat!' And she stomped off to meet the girls off the school bus.

'She sure is mad at him,' said Sam.

'He got mad at her too,' said Belle with a watery smile.

'Poor bloke.'

'Yes, but I get what Merrily means. I'd prefer to be questioned by Al. DI Steele is intimidating.'

'I'll see what I can do. I suppose there's no harm in asking.'

* * *

That night, Belle began having contractions. Sam raced her to hospital where she later lost the baby.

She spent the remainder of the night wide eyed and distressed as the blackness of her guilt engulfed her. Her poor baby!

The next morning Sam came to see her. She lay with her back to him.

'Honey, I'm sorry,' he said, touching her gently on her hunched shoulder.

'Not as sorry as me.' She turned to

stare bleakly at him. 'I feel so guilty, Sam!'

'Why? This wasn't your fault, Belle.'

'I didn't love him enough.'

'Who? Your husband?' He looked confused.

'Well, him too, but no, my baby. I resented him.' And her large tawny eyes filled with tears and she started to cry.

Sam gathered her to him and rocked her back and forth. 'It's OK, Belle, it's OK. You're bound to feel bad. Just cry it out, honey.'

'But you don't understand. Xander wanted another baby. He thought it would help our marriage. He ... he forced me when I refused.' She sobbed even harder. 'I didn't want another baby. I knew it wouldn't help us.' Her voice ended on a note of desperation.

'Oh, Belle. Hush. I'm so sorry.'

'But my baby was conceived under pain and sufferance. I was so angry at Xander.'

'Yes, of course, but not the baby.'

'Yes, the baby too. And now he's gone

250

and I feel so desperately guilty.'

'Maybe it's not such a bad thing, you know,' said Sam, treading carefully. 'Maybe you would always have looked at that child and felt the anger and resentment?'

'I doubt it. My girls were conceived the same way,' she said flatly. 'But I love them anyway.'

'Oh my poor, poor girl!' And he held her closer.

'Xander was always demanding, always controlling. I didn't want to come to Australia. I didn't want to leave my family. But we always did what Xander wanted. It's how he got his jollies — being in control, being a bully. I don't blame the police for thinking I killed him. Even my mum thought I had! But he deserved it. He wasn't a nice man these past few years.' And she went off into another bout of crying.

'Belle, listen to me. It's important.'

Belle raised her head but stayed mute, her face wet and blotchy, but beautiful in Sam's opinion.

'My dad was like that,' he said.

Belle stared at Sam. 'But the beautiful willows and the water hole . . . '

'Oh, yes, he could do good things, but he liked to control with a fist of iron. Us four children were conceived through violence, but Mum gave us as much love as she had in her. She instilled in us good qualities.'

Belle raised her hand to touch his cheek.

He took it and kissed her palm and then said, 'When the old man died, my mum replaced him with my step-dad and he was just the same — even worse, because he had no love for those that weren't his own spawn. Those were his words. So don't beat yourself up, Belle. Mum loved us. You love your kids. That's all that matters. Life can turn out good after a bad start. We can make it happen . . . if you want it to.'

'I want it to. I really do.'

'I'm glad to hear it.' And he raised her hand for another kiss.

She pulled it away. 'But there are other

things you need to know about me, things that may change how you feel . . . '

'I won't change. But tell me later, when you feel stronger and less emotional. Now sleep.' And he kissed her tenderly. 'You need to rest.'

15

Rhys Steele arrived at the Taggarts' farm mid-afternoon. He'd already visited Belle Bright's cottage but no one was home. He had to find her. Confront her face-to-face and see her reaction to the next piece of incriminating evidence. The woman was a good actress, he'd give her that.

Dotty greeted him first, bounding across the courtyard. Oh, great. The Taggart Termagant was at home. He held up his hand and commanded the Lab to sit within three metres of him. The obliging mutt sat. Well, at least one female in the vicinity obeyed him.

'I don't know how you have the gall to even show your face here!' came a searing voice from the house.

Steele couldn't see her, but the voice and the stridency were pure Merrily Taggart.

'Good afternoon, Ms Taggart,' he said.

Just what was her problem with him?

'I'm looking for Belle Bright.'

'Really.' He nodded. She was acting like some kind of guard dog! 'She's at the hospital.'

Steele had a cold premonition that Milo had surfaced and done her damage. 'She OK?' he asked, steeling himself for a negative answer.

'No. She's had a miscarriage. Straight after your damn interview. How does that make you feel, DI Steele? Happy that you got a result?'

'I'm sorry. I didn't know she was pregnant.'

'You're a 'tec. What happened to your highly trained powers of observation? But oh no! You had to go charging in like the proverbial bull among the fragile china.'

Merrily Taggart stepped out of the shadows of the verandah looking mad. 'And now she's lost the baby. Well done you!'

'Hey, lady, I apologise, but that wasn't my fault. This is a murder investigation and I was doing my job to the best of my ability.'

'Well, your job sucks!'

'Yeah, well it does sometimes. Nothing is perfect. Stuff happens. So get off my case.'

He left to swing by the local cop shop and see Al Tonkin. They needed to search the cottage.

* * *

'You can go home but just take it easy,' said the doctor. 'And I would suggest you make an appointment with one of the doctors in town before too long. Your blood pressure is high and your iron count low. You need to get yourself back in shape, Mrs Carlson.'

'We'll need to stop at the shops on the way home,' Belle said diffidently once they got in the ute. 'I'll need to stock up on some things before we get out to the farm.'

'I'm pretty alright for everything,' said Sam.

'But I'm not.'

'OK, but tell me what you need and I'll go in and get it. You heard the doc — you're not meant to be on your feet for too long.'

They parked outside the supermarket and Sam turned inquiringly to Belle.

She blushed, embarrassed. 'It's best if I go in. I have to get some, er . . . female stuff.'

'Oh.' Sam scratched his head. 'Well, you can't. I'll just have to do that for you. Just tell me what you need.'

'But . . . '

'Hey, OK, it's cool, really. I won't be long . . . '

He found the right aisle with difficulty and then gazed blankly at what was on offer. Good grief, what sort? He threw a few different types and brands into the trolley and made a rush for the check-out — before he was spotted by any of his poker mates!

The girl at the checkout raised her eyes to his.

'You in transition, Sam?' she said,

straight faced, as she efficiently scanned the feminine hygiene products.

'You know how it is,' he said, not quite so efficiently ramming the packets into bags.

'Cosmetics are on special today. Just saying . . .'

'You're funny, Angie, you know that?'

'Oh, I know it!' And she giggled as she took his money and handed over the change.

★ ★ ★

Belle waited in the ute for Sam. Feeling miserable and far too hot for comfort, she cranked open the passenger door to see if there was any breeze. There wasn't, but she left the door open anyway, in a vain hope one would come by and give her some relief.

As the minutes ticked on, she idly watched the flow of locals going about their daily business. One or two gave her a friendly wave, others a nod of recognition. Even though she'd tried to keep a low profile, she'd still managed to get to know quite a few of the town folk. So much for keeping her head down and being invisible. She'd had rocks in her head, coming to this small, close-knit community.

Then the indomitable Patty Clarke came into view. Bother! That woman had no filter.

'Ria, dear,' said Patty, making a bee-line for her. 'What's been going on? I heard you were in hospital? Nothing too serious I hope?'

'Oh, you know, women's things,' Belle said evasively. She had no desire to go into details because then everyone and their dog would know her sorry business.

'I can see you're embarrassed, dear. Don't be. We all have these issues. I must say, though, it's so lovely to see you and Sam together. I thought you'd get on well. I sense these things, you know.'

'We're just neighbours,' protested Belle, but without much conviction.

'You're so sweet,' laughed Patty. 'Your smooch in the high street the other day didn't go unnoticed. It's been the talk of the town.'

Oh boy! Belle hadn't given it a thought that the street kiss would come back to bite her.

'We were just messing about,' she said lamely.

'Of course you were, dear. There's nothing wrong with that. Oh, to be young and in love!'

'Yes, well . . . ' There was nothing Belle could think of to say.

She wished Sam would hurry up so she could escape this nutty woman. She glanced over to the supermarket entrance to see if he was as the checkout. He wasn't and she resigned herself to a further period of gossip torture.

Her gaze then fell on a thickset man sitting on the jarrah bench by the community noticeboard. He had a small white fluffy dog that was barking with big attitude at anybody who went past.

'That dog's got sass,' she remarked to Patty as the woman took a much needed breath.

'Horrible yappy thing,' said Patty. 'He never keeps it on a lead.'

'It's doing no harm. Ah. Here comes Sam.' At last! She could see him chatting to the checkout girl. 'Nice seeing you, Patty. But we've got to go.' Belle shut the door to effectively terminate the conversation and so, undeterred, Patty turned her attention to Sam.

As Belle waited for Sam, she glanced back at the dog. She smiled at its antics and raised her eyes to the owner. Their eyes locked. He smiled too. And her blood froze.

Belle gasped. Quickly she locked her door and raised her hand to shield her face. Between her fingers, she saw Sam loping towards the ute. The man stood up as if to come over to speak to her. Sam tried opening the door as she fumbled to unlock it. He swung it open and leaned into the cab. 'Hey, Belle? What's going on? You're white as a sheet.'

'I . . . I'm fine,' she stuttered. 'But get in quick. We have to go.'

'What?'

'Now. Please! Move it!'

As he moved around to the driver's side, Belle relocked her door. The man had stopped but was still staring, still smiling.

Then he blew her a kiss.

That was when Belle knew, knew for sure.

Sam got in and fired up the engine.

'I can turn around and go back to the hospital if you're feeling unwell?' he said.

'No. it's not that. Just get going. Take me to the police station. Fast!'

He swung out into the high street and headed towards the small brick police station.

As he drove, he said, 'Now are you going to tell me what the hell is going on? Anything to do with your chat with Patty?'

He flicked her a glance. She had her eyes tightly closed and she looked as if she was going to be sick. 'And you're sure you don't want the hospital, Belle?'

'No. I need to see Al immediately. That man that was sitting outside the

262

supermarket — he was from Sydney.'

'What the old guy with the shiatsu?'

'Yes.'

Sam cracked a laugh. 'Yeah, I know. That was Bernie Cornish.'

'You know him?' Belle turned huge, incredulous eyes on him.

'Well, yes. He comes here once in a while to check on his property.'

'He lives here?' This was getting worse by every second.

'Not permanently. He's got a holiday place with several hundred acres on the other side of town.'

'Of course he does,' she said bitterly. 'What are the chances!'

'Why? What's the problem?' Sam frowned as he parked the truck outside of the station.

How could she tell Sam that Bernie Cornish was one of Milo's business contacts, that he had been one of her regular hostessing clients at the Singing Chimp?

Instead, Belle said, 'I think we need police protection.'

'Against Cornish? Do me a favour,

Belle! He's just an old bloke with a dog. How can he possibly be a threat?'

'He recognised me.'

Are you sure? You look so different now.'

She turned her head sharply towards him. 'How would you know that?'

'Because, Belle, honey, I Googled you and your picture came up. And very sweet you were too with your long dark hair. And you still are!' he added. 'I like the blonde look too.'

'You were researching me?' She demanded accusingly.

'Wouldn't you do some background digging if a fugitive — however cute — moved in next-door?'

'You thought I was cute?' And she suddenly smiled, in spite of everything.

'You know I did, and still do.' And he smiled too. 'And maybe he did recognise you. So what's the big deal?'

'He's a colleague of Camelo Milo.'

'Ah. Now I think I get it . . . sort of.'

★ ★ ★

Al wasn't at the station. They waited in a back room for what seemed hours, Belle sitting on an orange plastic chair while Sam paced up and down like a caged lion.

'This is madness,' said Sam, getting to the end of his tether. 'It's a total waste of time. Explain again why you need police protection when you have me to look after you? I can take down that old guy if he becomes a problem.'

'I don't want to put you in that position. You might get hurt.'

'Bernie Cornish couldn't hurt me.'

With that, Al came in the room. 'What's going on?' he said. 'What's all this about needing police protection?'

'I have to speak to you in private about that,' said Belle.

'Oh for heaven's sakes, Belle. I'm involved too now,' said Sam.

'Please, Sam.'

Al opened the door expectantly and titled his head. Sam rolled his eyes and stomped out of the room. 'This is ridiculous!' he said.

Al shut the door behind him and said,

'So what's all this about, Belle?'

She told him about Bernie Cornish and how she had met him when hostessing at the Singing Chimp, and that he'd recognised her in spite of her new look.

'He must have been listening to my conversation with Patty Clarke and recognised my voice, if not my appearance. He's really close with Milo. There's a very real chance he'll tell him he's seen me and that makes me so scared, Al. What if Milo comes here?'

'The trouble is, Belle, we don't have the resources to have around-the-clock protection. Stay with Sam. That's your best bet. And we'll swing by when we can.'

'And that's all you can do?'

'At this stage, yes. I'm sorry.'

'So am I,' she said bitterly.

It was tempting to take off with the girls again and just disappear, except she was too fragile with her health — and she owed it to Sam not to breach her bail conditions.

But it was tempting, all the same.

16

Al Tonkin arrived at the farm two days later. Sam saw him from where he was loading grain into the ute for the cattle. He leaned against the ute and watched. The cop sat in the patrol car for a good five minutes. He gave the impression he was psyching himself up. That didn't bode well.

Sam straightened up and strode over to the car. Al got out as he approached. He was lacking his usual bonhomie bounce.

'How's she doing?' he said to Sam, his expression grim.

'Sad and sore.'

'Look, I meant to say the other day, but I'm sorry about the baby, mate.'

'So am I.'

'These things happen. There'll be time to have more. Me and the wife lost a couple early on.'

'That was tough.'

'It was. But there's plenty of time to try again.'

'What are you saying, Al?'

'It was yours, wasn't it?'

'No!'

'But I thought . . . '

'Barking up the wrong tree, mate. It wasn't my kid. Belle and me haven't got that sort of relationship.'

Sam wondered how many more times he would deliver that line. Would he and Belle ever get to the point of an intimate relationship? Well, it wasn't looking hopeful from where he was standing.

Last night she'd told him about her work as a hostess. She seemed to think it would disgust him, but he didn't care. He loved her — yes loved her — for who she was, not for what she'd done. But her own self-disgust had become a barrier between them.

'Sorry. I thought you two were — but my mistake. Anyway I need to speak to her.'

'You're not here as security, then?'

'No.'

'I see. Can't it wait then? She's still in bed.'

'No. Steele's on my back to get this done as soon as. I don't think he's game to interview Belle at the moment, not since your sister gave him the what-for.'

'Good old Merry. But I can't think Belle can add anything new. You've pretty much grilled her on everything.'

'We've additional evidence, Sam.'

'Oh. Is this about Bernie Cornish?'

'No. We've nothing on him. He's clean as a whistle, which is what I expected.'

'Me too. He's a decent bloke. I think Belle's overreacting, but I guess she's rather sensitive at the moment. She's not thinking straight.'

'Yeah, well . . . I'm sorry, Sam but I don't think Belle is as innocent as she appears.'

'What do you mean?'

'Looks like she been laundering money through the town's retailers.'

Sam closed his eyes monetarily. OK then. And why wasn't he surprised? Because she'd had all that damned money stuffed in her freezer compartment, that's why! Well, things just kept getting crazier.

'Did you know anything about it, Sam? Because you don't seem fazed, mate.'

'I know she had a bundle of notes. I found them by accident.'

'Right. And you didn't think to tell me?'

'I thought it was her savings. But I didn't ask her because I didn't want to know.' And this only confirmed he'd made the correct decision. Money laundering! What next?

'Well perhaps it was her nest egg, except that counterfeit money has turned up in Mooralup and Busabarup. There aren't that many options for how it got into our community. We're not exactly high flyers in Mooralup, now are we? And then there's the little fact that the banknotes' serial numbers are compatible with dirty money from Sydney's nightspots, which were in turn part-owned by Camelo Milo. She's involved, Sam, like it or not. What can I say?'

'This is the pits. I'll go and see if she's

awake.'

Five minutes later, Al sat down next to Belle and gave a brief smile.

She was sitting on the sofa in a man's blue plaid dressing gown which Al presumed belonged to Sam. Her hair was spiky, her mouth was pulled down and unsmiling, her eyes large and wary, a questioning expression in their depths.

'Al . . . ' she said.

'How ya doing?'

'Not too bad, considering.'

'Well, look here, Belle, I know it's not good timing and you're not feeling too fit, but I need you to answer some more questions.'

'What else is there to say? I've told you everything I know.'

'It's about counterfeit money . . . '

She shot him a suspicious look. 'I don't know anything about counterfeit money.'

'I don't believe you, Belle,' he said sternly. 'Fake notes have been turning up at the Mooralup supermarket and roadhouse. Those notes have serial numbers that link them to fake money being circulated through nightspots in Sydney.'

'OK. Stop right there,' she said with a weary tone. 'I can see where this is going.' Her hand curled into a fist. 'This is about the money in the freezer compartment of my fridge. Did you tell him about it?' She looked accusingly at Sam.

'No. This has nothing to do with me. I didn't break your confidence.'

'OK, then. Sorry.' But she didn't sound happy.

'So you knew the money was fake?' said Al.

'No, but I'm probably the only person in Mooralup whose recently been in Sydney — apart from Cornish — so it's not exactly a quantum leap to conclude that my money is bad.'

'Where did you get it?'

She clasped her hands in her lap, twisting her fingers into the blue plaid material.

'I found it under the mattress of our bed on the day my husband died.'

'Right. That was a coincidence.'

'It's true, Al. I was making the bed earlier that morning. I found it as I tucked in the bottom sheet. I took it to the office to confront him, to ask him where he'd got it.'

'I thought you'd gone there to ask him to sign your divorce documents?'

'Well, yes. But I hadn't intended to go and get his signature on that particular day. I'd been sitting on those divorce papers for a while, waiting for the right time. You can check with my lawyer. She was hassling me to get on with it.'

'Don't worry, we will.'

'Finding that money was the just the last straw,' Belle went on. 'I was so mad at Xander for having it. When Milo threatened me I decided to use the money to live under the radar. I didn't stop to even think if the money was clean or not. It didn't even occur to me that it wasn't. I was in survival mode. I couldn't use my own bank account in case you lot would track me. So I used the cash.'

'How much was there?'

'About ten thousand.'

Sam whistled through his teeth. Al flicked him an irritated look before re-concentrating on Belle. 'Is there much left?'

'Some. Maybe five grand or more. But it's not cheap, living on the run.' She gave the ghost of a weary smile.

'And it's still at the cottage?'

She nodded. 'And I've got about a hundred in my purse.'

'I need to bag all of it. Are you well enough to come to the cottage with me so you can oversee the seizure?'

'Is that a good idea?' said Sam. 'She's only just come out of hospital.'

Belle shrugged. 'I'll be OK, Sam. This needs to be sorted. I'll go and get dressed.'

'I'll make sure she's OK,' said Al.

'To hell with that. I'm coming too.'

★ ★ ★

As they approached the cottage, they saw Steele leaning laconically against his car under the shade of the giant oak tree. He looked cool and aloof in his blindingly white shirt and tailored black trousers, and Belle hated him on sight.

She sucked in a sharp breath and her hand instinctively shielded her belly. 'He's got a nerve. What's he doing here?'

'His job,' said Al bluntly. 'Come on, Belle. The sooner we get this done the better.'

Belle reluctantly got out the car and walked tautly towards the cottage, ignoring the DI when he stepped forward to greet her.

'I'm sorry about the baby, Mrs Bright,' he said. 'Truly sorry.'

Belle marched on, blanking him.

Steele dropped his hand with a shrug. At least he'd tried. He followed the others at a distance.

Belle unlocked the back-door and entered the stuffy, neglected kitchen that smelled of mouse and decaying fruit. She'd only been gone a few days but the place felt sad and unloved.

'Oh god,' she said. There was a catch in her voice. 'Look!'

The green kitchen table was dusty and bare except for one item; a rock sat squarely at its centre. And not any old rock, either, but one brightly painted with white and yellow daisies.

'Well, well . . .' said Steele from the open doorway. 'Who would have thought? Our missing rock appears after all this time.'

'That means Milo's already here!' Belle gave a nervous sweep of the room as if she would find him lurking in a dark corner.

'Or perhaps you put the rock there to make it look like he is.'

'Why would I do that?' She angrily spun around to face Steele as he approached the table. 'I haven't seen that rock since that day.'

'So you say, Mrs Bright. But you were the only person who allegedly saw — and used — the rock in the first place. And there's been no sign of it till now.'

Ferociously she glared back at him. 'I promise you, I didn't plant the rock there. Milo is the only one who could have done that.'

'Why would he?'

'As a message to me, that he's finally found me, that he's knows exactly where I am.'

'You sound very convincing, Mrs Bright.'

'That's because it's true.'

'I still reckon you murdered the two men and you're using Camelo Milo as a smokescreen.'

'That's enough! Leave her alone, Steele,' growled Sam. 'Belle hasn't murdered anyone.'

Steele raised his brows questioningly. 'And you know that for a fact, Mr Taggart?'

Sam took an aggressive step forward and Belle pulled him back. 'Thanks, but I can fight my own battles, Sam,' she said.

Then she faced Steele, standing only centimetres away, and said, 'You,' she poked Steele centre chest of his spotless white shirt, 'should question Cornish, and get off my back.'

'Who's Cornish?'

'I told Al about him. I saw him two days ago. He's one of Milo's cronies and it's no coincidence that he saw me in the street and then this happens.' She stabbed a finger at at the rock. 'He must have tipped off Milo. He knows where Milo is, or at least how to contact him. You follow it through, DI Steele, and arrest that man who murdered my husband before he hurts any more of my family!'

'Cornish is clean,' interrupted Al. 'I meant to tell you about him, sir. We've done a check on him already.'

'No — he hangs out with Milo,' said Belle.

'Come on, Belle. He's a respected businessman. He's invested a great deal of money in this region, what with his vineyards and avocado orchards,' said Sam. 'He employs a lot of locals and sponsors community initiatives.'

'He's still a crook,' said Belle flatly.

'Look, let's just get the money, Belle, and then you can go back with Sam and rest,' Al said.

'I'll bag the rock,' said Steele. 'I'll get it tested for prints and DNA, though it's probably been wiped clean.' He shot Belle a challenging look. 'What do you think, Mrs Bright?'

'How would I know?' Belle refused to rise to the bait. Instead she stepped over to the fridge and retrieved the plastic bag of money from the small freezer compartment. She handed it to Al.

'Is that everything?' he said.

'Yes.' Then her eye flickered ever so slightly as she belatedly remembered the key she'd buried in the dripping pot. But she was loathe to hand it over. It could be a bargaining chip with Milo if things got bad. 'You can take a look yourself to be sure.' She stepped away from the fridge.

Al rummaged around the freezer and then the fridge. Belle realised she was holding her breath, hoping he wouldn't mine the dripping pot. She tried to surreptitiously silently exhale. Al moved on to her pantry and then the kitchen cupboards. Again he didn't find anything that interested him.

'I'm all done here. Let's take you back to the farm,' said Al.

'Is it OK if we empty the fridge and take back the perishables with us?' Belle asked.

'No. Al needs to drop you off and get to Busabarup by lunchtime.'

'OK.' She wasn't happy. She wanted that key.

* * *

Steele watched them leave and then wandered back into the kitchen. He stared at the fridge. There was something in that fridge that Belle Bright wanted. What had she hidden in there? Well, there was only one way to find out. He rolled up his sleeves and began a systematic search of the foodstuffs, spreading them out on the table and emptying every packet and cannister.

The dripping had melted by the time he got to it. He stuck his fingers in the thick, gloopy fat and encountered the key.

'Well, well, Mrs Bright,' he said to the empty kitchen. 'What does this little gem open, wonder? And why didn't you want us to find it?'

He put the key in a evidence bag and then put everything back in the fridge as he'd found it.

17

Sam was out on the farm and Merrily had taken the girls to meet the school bus. Belle was on her own in the old cottage at last. She pushed her fingers into the dripping and felt around. The key wasn't there! What? But it must be. No one could have taken it. No one else knew it was in there. She fished around again to make sure.

'What are you doing, Belle?'

Belle jumped. Merrily was standing a few feet away, her arms crossed, regarding her coolly. Belle cast around for an explanation.

'Don't even think about lying to me, Belle. You may have got my brother duped, but not me.'

'I haven't duped him,' she protested.

'You've constantly withheld information and been economical with the truth. He's now stuck in this toxic situation. It's not fair on him.'

'It's not my fault. I warned him to keep away from us, that we were trouble.'

'Which would have appealed all the more to his chivalric nature. Oh, you've played him well.'

'I didn't play him! He wanted to help us.'

'I don't want you hurting him, Belle.'

'I don't want to hurt him. I care about him.'

'So be upfront with the police. Tell them everything. And I mean everything. Trust Al. He's a decent bloke.'

Belle knew Merrily was justified in her anger. Belle had embroiled Sam in all of this. She should have been stronger. She should have gone to the police straight away, right from the very start, regardless of Milo.

'You're right,' she said on a sigh. 'I've made such a mess of things.'

'So I'll ask you again, what were you doing?'

'I'd hidden a key in the fat. It's not there now.'

'And this key is important?'

'I guess . . . I don't really know.' She went over to the sink and washed the dripping off her hands. 'I found it in an envelope with the money and I hid it, just in case.'

'You'd best tell Al and if you don't, I will.'

Dotty began barking. There was a roaring command for her to sit.

'Sounds like my least favourite cop has arrived. I'll make myself scarce and you can tell him rather than Al — and make sure you do.'

Merrily slipped from the room, passing DI Steele. 'She's in there,' she said bluntly and disappeared.

Steele came in and glanced at the muck on the table. 'Looking for this, by any chance?' He held up the silver-coloured key.

'You had it! But how come?'

'You're not much of a liar, Mrs Bright. You gave yourself away wanting to clear the fridge. So what can you tell me about this key?'

Belle gave him the scant details.

'And that's it?'

'I don't recognise it from home,' said Belle. 'I've no idea if it belonged to Xander or Milo. Or anybody else for that matter.'

'Well, we've got a warrant to search your Sydney house.'

'Is that necessary?'

'I think so. I want you to be there when we do the search.'

'Go to Sydney? But what about my girls?'

'They'll be looked after here. We won't be gone for long. It'll be a quick round trip. We'll leave tonight and be back by tomorrow evening.'

* * *

It was confrontational rocking up to the Sydney house. The lawn was unkempt, the driveway littered with autumn-yellow London plane leaves and rubbish. There must have been a dust storm during her absence, as a red veneer had settled over the outdoor furniture and window. Inside the house wasn't much better. The air was stale and the rooms chaotic. Steele had been right; someone had ransacked it.

The DI and three other officers systematically worked their way through the house, making the mess worse, while Belle sat on the lounge and tried not to cry at the depressing scene. She itched to tidy up but was told not to touch anything. The whole place needed to be packed up, and the house sold so she could close this chapter of her life. Bring on the day. It couldn't happen soon enough.

She wasn't surprised when Steele announced that the key didn't fit any of the locks at the house.

'Did your husband belong to a gym or a sports club? Or any social clubs?' he asked.

'He may have. I'm not sure. He didn't share that side of his life with me.'

One of the officers was going through paperwork. 'Hey, boss, this might be something,' she said. 'It's membership of a country club in the Blue Mountains,

Sky Sanctuary. Looks expensive.'

'Oh. We went there with Milo when we first arrived in Sydney,' said Belle. She frowned, remembering. 'Actually I think we were introduced to Nat Thomas there. I'd forgotten that. I knew the name was familiar but I couldn't place it at the time.'

'Convenient you've only remembered now,' said Steele.

'It wasn't a big deal. He was just at the bar. We didn't talk long. In fact I barely spoke to him at all, so get off my back, DI Steele.'

As it was, Sanctuary Sky came up trumps: Xander and Milo were members, Cornish owned the premises and employed Thomas as his assistant, and the key fitted a locker that was registered in Xander's name. Inside was a soft sports tote full of money, about half a million dollars worth.

'Score,' said Steele. 'Looks like we should be talking to Cornish.'

'Way overdue in my opinion,' muttered Belle.

Steele drove Belle back to Sam's farm. The sky was pastel pink and streaked with silver. The first birds were piping their dawn refrains and a chill autumn stillness held the land. The house, too, was hushed.

Belle tiptoed into the kitchen as the red tail lights of the cop car disappeared from view. She was dead on her feet and yearned for her bed but first she needed a drink of water and a painkiller. Her head was splitting.

It was then she spied the bear.

Elspeth's toy teddy was propped up on the table. Belle stared, her heart in her mouth. She hadn't seen that yellow teddy for months because they'd left it behind in Sydney.

Oh god! Her blood thrummed as she reach for the bear. There was a note tied around it's neck: *You've got what I want and I've got what you want. Meet me at the cottage. Alone.*

Belle sucked in a panicked breath.

Had he taken her girls!

She flew into their bedroom. Both beds were empty, their sheets thrown back untidily.

Belle raced back to the kitchen and scrawled a brief note to Sam.

She snatched her car keys and fled to the cottage with no other thought than that she had to protect her daughters.

She drove too fast along the gravel road, skidding on the corners. The Holden wasn't built for speed but Belle did her best to keep on track.

Her mind was whirling like an angry twister, full of fury and destruction. She was sick to the pit of her stomach.

How long had Milo had the girls? So much for them being kept safe! She cursed Steele for taking her away, and the police and the Taggarts for not protecting her precious babies!

She parked haphazardly under the oak tree, next to a black BMW, and ran to the cottage. There was a photo pinned smack in the middle of the door. It was of her and Xander in dinner dress with

RIP written in thick black ink across their faces. The rat!

She wrenched it off the door, scrunching it into a ball and chucking it on the floor.

The house was quiet. She listened hard for the sound of breathing, for any indication that her daughters were there. But there was nothing. Just a wall of silence.

'I know you're here, Milo!' she yelled. 'Give me back my girls!'

'Mummy?' The clear sweet voice of her daughter called out to her.

'Elspeth! Darling, where are you?'

The child whimpered.

The house was small and Belle wasted no time checking the rooms. But there was no one there. 'Where are you, baby? Hannah? Girls!'

There was only crying. It got louder and the next moment Milo was standing at the open front door. He held a gun in one hand and a phone in the other. He turned off the phone's recording; the crying abruptly stopped.

'Gotcha, Belle Bright,' he said and laughed as he slipped the phone into his trouser pocket.

'Where are my girls?' she demanded.

'All in good time. My, but you've played me a merry dance. I'm surprised you gave me the slip for so long.'

'How did you find me? Was it Cornish?'

'That was a lucky break. I'd been despairing till then.' Milo shook his head. 'Really, what were the odds that you'd end up in his stomping ground? Karma, my dear girl. What can I say? It was all meant to be.'

'I want my girls.'

'And I want my money,' he retaliated fast, his smile disappearing. 'Now.'

'It's in a safe place.' She couldn't tell him that the police had it!

'Ah, that's what your dear husband said after he stole it from me. I do hope you're not going to do the same, Belle?'

'You get the money when I get my girls back.'

'Big words, Belle darling, but how are you going to deliver, hmm?'

He saw her apprehension and made a grab for her arm, twisting it hard, causing her to cry out. 'Where is it? And don't lie to me. I know Bright had it stashed somewhere.'

Fear swamped her, paralysing her. 'I haven't got it!' she blurted out.

He wrenched her around and frog-marched her outside to the back garden. The sky was now a rosy red, setting the clouds on fire with its brilliance. But the beauty was lost on Belle. It reminded her of blood.

Milo pushed her on to the ground, forcing her to her knees. Dead prickly grass and small stones dug into her flesh, but that was the least of her worries. The unwavering gun pointed at her head eclipsed everything.

'Then where is it?'

'The police found it. In a locker. At the Sanctuary Sky Country Club.'

'Damn pommie! I should never have made him a member. You caused all this trouble, you know,' he said bitterly.

'What do you mean? I didn't take your money.'

'But it was because of you that Bright stole it, trying to impress his hard-to-please, cold-hearted missus. He wanted to keep you sweet with an expensive life-style because you were unhappy.'

'I never asked for that! I just wanted his love and fidelity, which he was incapable of giving. Besides, I doubt he stole the money for me. I know about his affairs.' She took a deep breath. 'What about my girls? Where are they?'

'You don't deserve to see your daughters again. You tried to kill me,' he said, no longer sounding reasonable.

'Oh, please! I hit you with a pebble. It wasn't life threatening.'

'It hurt all the same.'

'I'm so sorry.'

His eyes narrowed. 'I don't think you are. You left me to die.'

'Let me clarify, Milo. I'm sorry I didn't hit you harder and kill you!' she shot back.

His hand flew out and he hit her across the head with the side of the gun. Belle sunk to the ground on a sob, clutching her forehead with both hands as she skimmed the dirt.

'Rat!' she said through clenched teeth as blood welled through her fingers.'What are you going to do? Shoot me, like you did Xander and Thomas?' She raised her head and glared at him. The blood trickled down the side of her face. She felt impotent, terrified she was going to die without saving her girls. She tried to think how she could protect them, but she was at a loss.

'Let my babies go. They've done you no harm,' she pleaded.

'They're mine now. I'll do with them whatever I want. I'll have plenty of clients willing to pay for their services. It'll make up for the lost money.'

Suddenly, all the shame of those days came flooding back and Belle saw red. She sprung at him, flinging her body against his, clawing and kicking and punching.

'You're not having my girls, you monster!'

They fought bitterly, but Milo was bigger and stronger. He held her down face-down, grabbed her hair and twisted it ruthlessly so her head was forced up at a harsh angle, causing her to gasp in pain as she spluttered and spat out dirt. Belle shut her eyes, wishing that he would just shoot and get it over with. She'd had enough. She couldn't beat him, couldn't fight him.

He lifted the gun.

A shot rang out.

* * *

Sam's roar woke Merrily suddenly. 'Call the police!' he yelled.

'What?' Merrily shuffled sleepily out of her bedroom, pulling on her robe. 'Goodness, my head's killing me. What was in that wine? I thought it was organic?'

'Focus, Merry! Call the police. The girls are gone! Kidnapped or something.

295

Belle's gone off to the cottage after them.' He thrust the teddy into her hands. 'I'm going too.'

Two cars were parked under the oak. One was Belle's old brown bomb, the second was a smart black BMW.

Sam's ute skidded to a halt next to the beamer. He dashed a hand across his blurred eyes and shook his head to try and clear it. Dammit, he felt as groggy as hell. The wine must have been spiked. He scrambled out the ute cab, taking his .22 rifle with him. He loaded the gun and stuffed extra bullets into his shirt pocket.

The old house was quiet. No parrots chattered in the rosemary bushes. No crows bossily cawed in the gums. Even the feral marmalade cat was nowhere to be seen.

Sam prided himself on being a pragmatic down-to-earth man, but he could have sworn the hairs on the back of his neck rose a good six inches heavenwards as he crept through the rooms to the back verandah.

He caught a snatch of voices on the breeze. He clenched his jaw and tightened his grip on the gun. Cautiously, trying his best not to make a sound, Sam followed the path to the outside laundry and toilet. He stopped, sucking in a sharp breath.

Belle was cowering on her knees in the dirt. Her blonde head was shoved forwards, held down by the barrel of a hand gun by a man in black casual trousers and tight black shirt.

The man was hanging over Belle and laughing in a way that made Sam's skin crawl.

Sickened, Sam hitched up his own gun, wondering what the hell he should do now. He wasn't into shooting people, though he felt he could make an exception; this man was nothing but vermin and Sam was used to shooting vermin.

He rubbed his eyes again to clear his vision. He felt his head had been stuffed full with cotton-wool. Damn that smooth talking Cornish. Belle had been right, he was rotten to the core!

Before Sam could shoot, Belle lunged at the man and fought him like a wildcat. But after a short scuffle, the man held her back down in the dirt. He wrenched her head and swung his gun.

Sam wasted no more time; he aimed and fired.

Screams rent the air. Sam bounded towards Belle and her attacker. Milo was clutching his arm, howling in pain. Before Sam could reach them, Belle had rolled away from Milo and scrabbled to pick up his fallen gun. She relaunched herself at the injured man and hit his injured arm hard so hard he yowled again.

'Tell me where my girls are or I'll shoot you,' she said, standing up unsteadily and waving the gun at him.

'Hey, Belle, take it easy,' said Sam. 'I've got him covered. Settle down. It's over.'

'Butt out, Sam! He's got my girls.' She aimed the gun at Milo's leg.

Milo spat in the ground and answered with a torrent of abuse.

Belle squeezed the trigger. The bullet hit the ground close to his knee, flicking up dried mud. He screamed again. 'You tramp!'

'Tell me or I will kill you,' she said.

Sirens wailed on the chill morning air.

'Wait for the police,' said Sam. 'Let them deal with it.'

Belle ignored him and shot closer to Milo, missing his knee by a hair's breadth. He began babbling, 'The boot,' he said. 'They're in the boot. For god's sake, get her away from me!'

'The key,' demanded Belle and fired again, this time narrowly missing his foot.

'In my back pocket!'

Belle lunged for the trousers before Sam could stop her. Milo snaked out his good arm and got her in a headlock, ripping the gun from her grasp. Sam waded in, trying to snatch at the the gun.

'Police! Stand down!'

Another shot rang out and Steele roared as he flung himself on top of the melee and pinned Milo in the dust, twisting his arm hard up his back so he couldn't use the gun again.

'You're under arrest, Camelo Milo,' said DI Steele — and then he passed out!

* * *

Al Tonkin rocked up to the Mooralup Hospital with a smile on his face. 'We've arrested Cornish,' he announced to the dishevelled group of patients. 'And he's admitted to money laundering. He claims he'd regularly used Milo to deal with the money distribution through his various nightclubs and bars. When he discovered half a million had gone missing, he got narky and took matters into his own hands.'

'Did he kill Xander?' asked Belle, surprised. She was sitting on a chair between her sleeping daughters' beds. She had a bandage on her forehead, another on her arm, and swathe of cuts, scratches, bruises and a black eye. Her jeans and T-shirt were dirty and torn and she looked absolutely exhausted.

'No, Belle. He sent his man, Nat Thomas, to work for Milo and Bright to find out what was going on. Thomas worked out that Milo was creaming off money from Cornish's profits and that Bright had realised the con and was in turn stealing that stolen money from Milo. I tell you, there really is no honour among thieves.'

'So who killed my husband?' said Belle.

'Milo. He's confessed. He said that Cornish was hounding him for the money and he was angry when he discovered Thomas had been spying on him. He shot him and then confronted Bright. They had a fight and he shot him too. And then you turned up.'

'I'm so glad it's finally over,' said Belle, her gaze resting on her girls. They had been found unharmed, but hot and sleepy, in the BMW boot. Apart from being drowsy from the sedatives Milo had given them, they were fine.

'Hey Sam, Cornish also admitted he

drugged you and Merrily with the wine he'd brought around,' said Al. 'He did it so Milo could take the girls and trade them for the cash which meant he would get his money back.'

'I can't believe we were so gullible,' said Merrily from her window seat. 'He said it was an apology for tipping off Milo about Belle. It was a nice drop of stuff, too.'

'We failed you, Belle,' said Sam, his voice low and regretful. He came over and hunkered down by Belle, taking her hand in his.

'Don't be silly,' She gazed earnestly into his eyes. 'You couldn't have known Cornish was going to do that. You liked the man. You had no reason to believe otherwise.'

'I should have listened to you. You did warn us about him.'

'Don't beat yourself up. I should have done so many things differently. Like going to the police when I first found Xander and not running away.'

'But then I wouldn't have met you.'

'True.' Belle smiled at him and squeezed his hand. 'So it's all worked out alright in the end.'

'Thanks to Steele.'

'Not only Steele. You were there, my hero.'

'Looks like the DI will be out of action for a while,' said Al.

'Oh? Was he hurt?' said Merrily.

'Yes. Didn't you know?

'No. Was he hurt bad?'

'He got shot in the leg while these two were wrestling with Milo. But he helped saved the day regardless.'

'I still don't understand why he was there,' said Belle. 'He'd told me he was driving back to Busabarup.'

'He was,' said Sam, 'But he told me he'd got a bad feeling, so he turned back towards the farm and then I came hooning by so he turned tail again and followed me.' Sam cradled her cheek with his other hand. 'But I think we were doing just fine. We were sure whipping Milo's ass.'

'I think we were too.'

'You're a devil when you get riled. Do you know that, honey?'

'Haha. You best remember that in future,' And they grinned at each other, in total accord.

Al cleared his throat. 'Looks like you're preparing for a life with cake, Sam,' he said with a chuckle.

'I don't understand,' said Belle.

'It's a long story . . . ' said Sam.

'I'm off so Sam can explain,' said Al. 'Come on Merry, let's leave the love-birds to it.'

As they left, Sam leaned in for a long kiss.

'I predict,' said Al, closing the door on them. 'That those little girls are going to make mighty fine bridesmaids a little down the track.'

'And me,' said Merrily punching him on the arm with a laugh. 'I want to be a bridesmaid too.'

★ ★ ★

DI Steele lay in his hospital bed. It was a week on and he was bored and sore. Not a good combination. He needed to be up and about to help tie up the investigation. This inactivity was getting to him. As was the pain.

There was a commotion outside his room. What was going on? Whatever it was, there was a lot of laughter and shrieks. And was that a bark?

The next minute, a black explosion of legs, tail and ears bounced into Steele's room, attached by a leash to her owner.

Dotty bounded up to the bed.

'Sit!' exploded Steele. The pain would be indescribable if that stupid mutt jumped on his injured leg!

'Down!' yelled Merrily. 'Sorry. She's excited about being here,' she apologised in a rush. Dotty skidded to a halt and barked her welcome. 'Quiet!' Steele commanded. The dog grinned.

'Stupid dog. Why did you bring her here?'

'She missed you and wanted to cheer you up.'

'You're projecting.'

'I am most definitely not. But I would like to say how grateful I am that you helped save the day. You were quite the man of the moment.'

'It's my job.'

'Well, good job, DI Steele. Well done.' And she made to leave.

'Is that it? Now you're going?'

'Yep. You don't want me to stay, do you?' Steele could hear the saucy challenge in her voice.

'No,' he said emphatically.

'Thought not. Come on, Dotty.' Steele watched the door close. Actually, he should have said yes, but he was damned if he was going to admit that to Merrily Taggart!

Anyway, he would be seeing her again, at Belle and Sam's wedding in the spring. By then his leg should be completely healed which meant he could run if Termagant Taggart got too mouthy.

Or he could dance her into sweet submission. He grinned. That sounded just fine by him.